MW01634321

SHIELDING JOLENE (SPECIAL FORCES: OPERATION ALPHA)

DELTA FORCE - GENERATION NEXT, BOOK 1

JEN TALTY

Welcome to *The Next Generation* of Delta Force. This series will focus on the men and women related to Susan Stoker's characters in her *Delta Team* and *Delta Team Two* series. In this first book, we meet Michael "Cannon" Santoro whose brother is Tony Santoro from *Rescuing Aimee* from the *Delta Team* series. Making cameo appearances are Porter "Oz" Reed from *Shielding Riley* and Gage "Lefty" Haskins and his wife, Kinley, from *Shielding Kinley* in the *Delta Team Two* series.

To find out more about Serenity Bale Reddington, check out *Cove's Blind Date Blows Up!*

Thank you for taking the time to read *Shielding Jolene*. Check out my other series inside Susan Stoker's world: *the Airforce Fire Protection* series *and the Search and Rescue* series.

Now grab a glass of vino (or whatever your favorite drink is) and kick back, relax, and let the romance roll in!

Dear Readers,

Welcome to the Special Forces: Operation Alpha Fan-Fiction world!

If you are new to this amazing world, in a nutshell the author wrote a story using one or more of my characters in it. Sometimes that character has a major role in the story, and other times they are only mentioned briefly. This is perfectly legal and allowable because they are going through Aces Press to publish the story.

This book is entirely the work of the author who wrote it. While I might have assisted with brainstorming and other ideas about which of my characters to use, I didn't have any part in the process or writing or editing the story.

I'm proud and excited that so many authors loved my characters enough that they wanted to write them into their own story. Thank you for supporting them, and me!

READ ON!
Xoxo
Susan Stoker

To Susan. Thank you for being you. It's an honor and a joy to be a part of this world.

CHAPTER 1

Michael "Cannon" Santoro ducked his head into his brother's fridge and snagged a couple beers. No one had called him Michael since the fourth grade when he'd decided to become a human cannonball for a school project. It hadn't been a successful endeavor and he broke a leg and a wrist, but the emergency room doctor coined him the "Cannon" and his family, especially his brother Tony, had thought it the most hysterical thing he'd ever heard. Tony had refused to call his little brother anything but Cannon and so the name stuck. Even Cannon's parents started calling him that within a couple of months. Hell, Cannon wasn't sure anyone remembered what his given name had been.

And frankly, he didn't care. Cannon fit his personality better anyway.

He inhaled sharply, taking a moment to himself. He glanced around his brother's kitchen. Tony was the kindest, most caring man, and Cannon was honored to have him as his blood brother. They didn't come any better than Tony, and Cannon knew that his brother was there for him, even in his darkest hour. But sometimes it was hard to open up. Tony understood that and he gave Cannon space, but lately he'd been pushing Cannon to talk more about his feelings.

Cannon was tired of it. He'd been talking about what happened ever since he'd returned from his last mission which had put one of his team members in the hospital. The entire deployment had been hard. One the most difficult assignments he'd ever been on since he joined Delta Force.

However, the truly hard part was that it should have been Cannon that was lying in that hospital bed, fighting to have some kind of life.

He blinked. He knew he needed to stop thinking like that. If the tables had been turned, Cannon would have done exactly the same thing for Skip. There was no question. The Army had trained them for the mission. Special forces was more than the mission. It was about the men as well and they took care of their own.

Skip took care of his team so they could complete the mission.

Cannon blew out a puff of air and cleared his mind. He headed through his brother's kitchen and out to the back patio where his brother Tony, his wife Aimee, and two other couples with a few kids were hanging out.

Cannon knew both Oz and Gage, whom everyone on the base called Lefty, from Delta Force. They weren't on the same team, but their paths had crossed more than a few times.

"Here you go." Cannon handed the cold brew to Lefty.

"Thanks, man." Lefty clanked it against Cannon's longneck. "How's Skip doing?"

"I don't know how he does it, but he's always got a smile on his face." Cannon ran a hand across his freshly buzzed head. "Unfortunately, his days out in the field are over," Cannon said. "The doctor said even though he'll walk again, his body won't ever be the same and he'll need at least two more surgeries."

"Jesus. That sucks," Oz said. "I can't imagine. Last I spoke with him, he mentioned he plans on staying in the military. Is that still true?"

"That's what he says. He wants to work behind the scenes with intelligence and our CO says the Defense Secretary has been to see him." Cannon couldn't fathom sitting behind a desk doing that type of research work. He needed to be in the field and he'd always thought if and when the time came he could no longer perform his duties, he'd leave the Army for good.

No way could he sit on the sidelines.

"Wow. That's huge," Lefty said.

"He's an excellent field counter-intelligence officer, so I bet he'll be able to make the transition easily enough," Oz added. "And if someone that high up in the government is making house calls, he'll do just fine."

Cannon nodded, only he wasn't so sure. He'd seen other men leave the field, for whatever reason, and it didn't work out so well. He glanced toward his brother. Tony had left. And to be a schoolteacher, no less. He was happier than anyone Cannon knew. So, it was possible.

Just not for Cannon.

"How's the new team member working out?" Tony asked. "What's his name?"

"Huck. Our team has worked with him before, so he's an excellent fit. Although Skip will be sorely missed; even if he's working with us in a different capacity, it won't be the same." Cannon rubbed his aching shoulder. Physical therapy had helped him regain his strength and he'd be back to his old self in a couple more weeks.

Something that Skip would never be able to accomplish and that would always cause a bit of guilt in Cannon's heart. His military therapist constantly reminded him that it wasn't his fault and he absolutely had to stop taking responsibility for Skip's injuries.

If the tables were turned, Cannon wouldn't want Skip to have regrets about being able to walk, much less keep his job in Delta Force.

"How long will your team be able to stay stateside?" his brother asked. "I certainly have enjoyed having you around these last few weeks."

"We still have a week left of vacation." Cannon shrugged. "But now that our training with Huck is over and I've been cleared both physically and psychologically, your guess is as good as mine."

"I seriously don't miss those days." Tony raised his finger and pointed to all the kids playing. "I like this life much better."

"I still can't believe my big brother is a first-grade schoolteacher, married, and a dad. It's so weird." All of Cannon's life, he admired and wanted to be like Tony. He'd followed him into the military, but he didn't follow him out.

And he wouldn't.

But the family life? Cannon had changed his thinking on that subject.

However, one of the reasons Cannon struggled with what happened to Skip was he couldn't imagine what it would be like to be lying in a hospital bed with a career-ending injury and having a family to take care of.

But Skip seemed to take what happened in stride. He put a smile on his face and told his team he'd still always have their backs, just in a different capacity. Skip didn't get angry. He didn't become resentful. He simply accepted his fate and moved on.

He was a better man than most soldiers in his position.

Or perhaps the reality hadn't sunk in yet.

"He's the best damn teacher ever," Oz said. "Thanks to him, Bria thrived when she was in the first grade and he helped Logan adjust as well. We're very grateful."

"Agreed," Riley, Oz's wife, said as she handed him their newborn son and plopped herself into the chair next to her husband and let out an exasperated sigh. "I would have never been able to step into this role without Tony's help."

"You're a great mom." Tony tipped his beer. "And a natural."

"It's one thing to ease into it after being pregnant and learning it as you go," Riley said. "It's quite something else to all of a sudden be responsible for two kids."

"I have to agree with my wife on this one." Oz ran a hand across his chin. "It's been a steep learning curve, but we wouldn't change it for the world. Right, babe?"

Riley laughed. "No. We wouldn't. As a matter of fact, we're getting ready to take on some foster kids."

"On top of a newborn? Have you lost your mind?" Lefty smacked his old friend on the back. "Why am I not surprised?"

Cannon eased back in one of the Adirondack chairs and nursed his beverage. His mind kept wandering back to Skip. From the second that man blinked open his eyes after nearly being blown to bits, he'd remained positive. It didn't matter that the doctors were telling him he might not walk again. Or when he'd planted his feet on the floor and stood, but the medical professionals told him that without a doubt, he'd never see active duty again, he shrugged, smiled, and said *but I'm alive and I can still hug my wife and serve my country.*

That was something that Cannon wasn't sure he could do. If he were in a position where he couldn't perform his current duties, he wouldn't re-enlist.

But what would he do?

That was the million-dollar question that Cannon couldn't answer. Sitting behind a desk while in the military would be worse than torture. But the idea of being a civilian made Cannon's skin itch like his body was covered in poison ivy.

He rubbed his forearm.

"Where'd you go, little brother?" Tony's voice snapped Cannon back to the present.

"Nowhere." Cannon stared out into the back-yard. Logan, Oz's nephew, was tossing a baseball against a fence while his little sister was skipping rope and Tony's kids raced around in circles, giggling.

And that was another concept that Cannon had begun to ponder.

Family.

In the past, the idea of having a family hadn't even been on his radar. He didn't have time and he was too focused on his career.

Now, his position in Delta Force was still his

number one priority, but he wasn't sure it was all he wanted.

Or needed.

However, it was nearly impossible to balance both.

He'd watched many couples go through painful divorces because of the strains the military put on marriages. Those that did survive were generally not in special forces. Those that were, like Oz and his wife, or Lefty and Kinley, were unique.

Of course, many retired shortly after forming their families or transferred into different positions that kept them home.

And out of the action.

"You could have fooled me," his brother said. "You look as if you're a million miles away."

Cannon could never pull the wool over his brother's eyes, so there was no point in lying. However, Cannon didn't like being this vulnerable in front of other Delta Force members, especially when they weren't on his team and while he knew them well enough and trusted them with his life, he didn't want to share his deep emotional thoughts. Hell, he barely liked opening up to his brother sometimes.

"If you're worried about Skip and his decision,

don't be." Oz leaned forward, resting his arms on the table. "He's got a wife and they want to start a family. He's more than happy with his decision to step out of the field and into a desk job. Besides, your team and every other team out there needs a good man like Skip working intel here at home. He's not some greenhorn whose never been on a mission and is trying to feed us important information. No. He's been out there in the trenches with us and will be able to decipher intel better than anyone."

Cannon knew that Oz was spot-on. "It will be nice to have a familiar voice on the other end when me and my team are in enemy territory waiting for the thumbs-up."

"Amen to that, brother." Lefty nodded. "But I take it that's not really what's bothering you, is it, kid?"

Cannon really hated being called *kid*. At thirty-two, he was far from a child. But he got that he was a good ten or fifteen years, if not more, younger than anyone in this backyard, including his brother, and all of them had seen a hell of a lot more action than he had.

So far.

"I keep telling him what happened to Skip isn't his fault," his brother said.

"Don't talk about me like I'm not sitting right

next to you," Cannon muttered. He always hated it when Tony did that. "And I've had all the discussions I need to about this topic with the Army shrink." He reached for the chips, setting it in his lap, and hoarding the entire bowl. He resented that he sounded like an angry teenager. He'd passed the psychological exam. The doctor had deemed him fit to go back into active duty.

She'd told him that he'd have these residual feelings of guilt and that they were normal. However, he needed to learn to let them go. He couldn't allow those kinds of emotions to fester because if he did, they would hinder his ability to do his job and that wouldn't be good for him or his team.

"I've been where you are," Lefty said. "A buddy of mine saved my life, and it cost him both his legs."

"Jesus," Cannon muttered. "Where is he now?"

"He lives in Florida with his wife and two kids and constantly reminds me if he could go back in time, he'd do everything exactly the same because if he hadn't, we might all be dead," Lefty said. "And what good would that do anyone?"

"That's a good point," Oz said. "I've read the report and if Skip hadn't pushed you out of the way, setting off a chain reaction of events, giving everyone on your team a chance to regroup, things could have happened very differently and who knows how things could have gone down."

Cannon had heard this from his commander, his teammates, his shrink, and from his brother. Deep down, he knew it was more than true.

It was a fact.

And the mission was fucked up to begin with.

They were all lucky to get out alive.

Skip's actions not only saved Cannon, but they saved the entire team and allowed them to complete the task.

Cannon nodded. "I understand all this, and I get that I would have done the same thing." He leaned back and glanced toward the sky. This was a safe space and these men had seen some serious shit. If he couldn't be honest with his feelings here, he couldn't be honest anywhere. "I just don't know what I'd do if the tables were turned. I can't visualize myself doing anything other than what I'm doing right now."

"Most of us can't," Lefty said. "Not until something in our lives changes and when that happens, our perspective shifts."

"And it's not something you have to worry about too much." Oz stood and slapped his shoulder. "If you're ever faced with having to make a major change in your career, you've got support and you'll eventually figure it out for the simple reason you won't have a choice." Oz meandered into the house.

Cannon set the bowl of chips back on the center of the table. He'd had enough of this heavy conversation and welcomed anything else.

Except the thick silence that filled the backyard.

"Did you ask him?" Kinley leaned forward and practically whispered in Lefty's ear.

"Not yet." Lefty wrapped his arm around his wife. "We were wondering if you had any plans tomorrow and if you could do us a huge favor."

"I have a few errands to run, but that's about it. What do you need?" Having too much free time on Cannon's hands only promoted more intense thoughts that made him ponder what his life would be like if he couldn't be in the field with Delta Force. Those thoughts made him crazy and served only to remind him of his mortality. He seriously couldn't wait for his team to be deployed.

"Kinley has agreed to be interviewed about the Alleyway Strangler by a true crime novelist."

"Seriously? That's pretty cool." Cannon had heard all about Kinley and her role in bringing down a killer.

"I'm not so sure about that," Kinley said. "But I've

read this author's work and I'm quite impressed by how she handles the material and focuses on the victims and not the killer and while I generally don't like discussing what happened, Jolene Whittle handles these stories like no other author. I figure I can control my narrative if I tell my story to her instead of having someone write about this killer and make assumptions about me because I won't do an interview."

"That makes sense," Cannon said. "But how do I fit into this?"

"Jolene arrives tomorrow," Lefty started. "My team has training scheduled that I can't get out of and I don't want my wife having to deal with this alone, nor do I want this Jolene person wandering around Texas by herself, interviewing all our friends. I want someone to keep an eye on her at all times and help control this narrative."

"You want me to tail her?" Cannon asked.

"I want you to pick her up at the airport tomorrow and remained glued to her side until you put her back on a plane and back to wherever it is she came from." Lefty held up his finger. "And I want a report on her every move."

"I can do that, but why don't you trust her?"

"For starters, I don't know her," Lefty said. "But

I've heard she digs for the unknown and looks for the story that wasn't told. Actually, she told me she wants to ask around and she won't put anything in the book that we don't want, but I don't like her poking around without someone I know and trust standing right next to her."

"Does she know you're asking someone to be her bodyguard, so to speak?" Cannon asked.

"Sort of," Lefty admitted.

"Because my boss was involved with the killer," Kinley said, "I'm worried she's going to push hard on the rumors that I knew more before I reported my suspicions. Jolene is an excellent writer and right now probably the best true crime author in the business. But in one case she was working on, she ended up causing some problems for the police officers who made the initial arrest. In her defense, it turns out the cops were covering up their mistakes, but I don't want to turn my part of the story into something it's not, and I certainly don't want the few friends I have harassed."

"Besides, we know that everything that we did was on the up-and-up," Lefty said. "However, we can't have some of what we did in that book either because of my job and I just want someone to help manage that. Would you mind helping?"

"I'm happy to. How long is this Jolene person staying?"

"Five days," Lefty said. "At the most. And I understand you might be called away to the base for some reason and there's nothing we can do about that, but I'd really appreciate it if you could free up as much time as possible."

"I've got nothing going on, so for the next week, I'm all yours." Cannon looked forward to focusing on anything other than the previous mission.

He pulled up his cell and found his reader app. He searched for Jolene Whittle's latest book and tapped the one-click button. He wasn't a big reader, unless it was about cars and motorcycles, but tonight he'd become Jolene's biggest fan.

At least long enough to get a decent understanding of what made Jolene Whittle tick.

He took one look at her author picture and his pulse increased. The air escaped his lungs as if they were balloons that had been popped. He cleared his throat.

"Something wrong?" Lefty asked.

"No." He pounded the center of his chest as he tried to catch his breath.

"Did you just look up Jolene?" Kinley asked.

"That author picture of hers is why that whole sexy librarian look is such a big thing with you men."

Cannon's cheeks heated. He had to admit, the black-rimmed glasses with the dark hair pooled up in a ponytail on the top of her head with a few stray strands fanning her face was a turn-on, but it was her crystal-blue eyes that held him captive.

"You better treat this like a job." Lefty cocked his head and arched a brow. "And not a hookup."

"She's not my type." Cannon set his phone screen down on his lap. Lookswise, she was exactly the kind of woman he was attracted to. "I'm not into the bookworm kind of girl. I like more of an outdoorsy chick."

"If you read her bio, she's into kayaking, camping, hiking—"

Lefty interrupted his wife. "Why would you tell him that? I want him to keep an eye on her, not date her."

"Why not? They might make for a cute couple," Kinley said.

Tony laughed.

"This is not funny," Cannon mumbled. "Lefty, you have nothing to worry about. I'll be nothing but professional."

"Famous last words," his brother said, lifting his beer.

Cannon did his best to erase the memory of Jolene's image from his mind, but he found it impossible. There was something in that picture that connected to his soul, and he couldn't shake the feeling that Jolene was going to change his life.

CHAPTER 2

Jolene Whittle let out an exasperated sigh as she stuffed her duffel bag in the overhead bin, grateful she'd checked her suitcase. The layover had been shorter than anticipated and she'd ended up with only thirty-five minutes to race through the airport to make her connection to Killeen Fort Hood Regional Airport.

It was rare that Jolene splurged on a first-class ticket, but it wasn't every day that Kinley Taylor Haskins agreed to an interview. Actually, Kinley had not once spoken to anyone about what happened since she'd testified against the Alleyway Strangler. Jolene couldn't imagine what it had been like for Kinley, and she would do her best to tell her story with the utmost respect.

She held her cell in one hand while she tugged her seat belt across her waist and smiled at the man who occupied the next seat. He looked vaguely familiar, but so did the woman sitting behind her. They'd probably raced through the airport or stood in line together somewhere.

He looked her over with a little too much gusto and his smile was a little too inviting. She didn't believe she was all that much to write home about, but she knew she wasn't ugly. Normally, whenever she traveled, she never wore makeup or did her hair. But this time, because she was being picked up by an associate of Kinley's husband, she felt it was important to put her best foot forward.

Based on the way her seatmate was giving her the once-over, she wished she'd opted for sweats, dirty hair, and bags under her eyes.

The flight attendant handed her a glass of white wine.

"Thank you so much," she said.

"My pleasure. I'm such a huge fan. I hope you don't mind me asking, but would you sign my book once we get up in the air?" the flight attendant asked.

"I'd be happy to." Jolene would never tire of people noticing her for her work. Being an author, it didn't happen often, so when it did, she reveled in it.

She only wished it hadn't happened while a man was ogling her.

"Can I get you anything else?" the flight attendant asked, glancing between her and the man situated in the aisle seat.

"I'm all good." The man nodded.

"Me too." Jolene turned her attention to the window and sipped her cheap wine and fiddled with her cell. She had no idea why she bothered with the alcoholic beverage, except it was free and wasn't that half the point of traveling first class? Besides, she needed to calm down. This was going to be the interview of a lifetime. A career maker simply because Kinley had made it clear she'd never speak to the media. Kinley was giving Jolene the chance to write the only authorized version of her story and that was huge.

And of course, there was the man picking her up at the airport.

Cannon.

His picture had been driving her crazy ever since Kinley had sent it this morning. Jolene had never been that attracted to a man in a photograph before. She couldn't shake how she felt as though she could see right into Cannon's soul and that scared her because it made no sense.

"I have to ask," the man said. "Are you really Jolene Whittle?"

She jumped, dropping her cell between the seats. "In the flesh." She bent over. "Shit," she muttered.

"I love your work," he said. "I listen to your podcasts all the time and I just downloaded your last book. You've come a long way from your days as a reporter." He reached between the seats, his fingers brushing up against hers.

She jerked her hand away. "What do you know about those days?"

"I went to the University of Virginia for both undergrad and medical school and I did my residency there. That's when your crime column came out and I used to read it every week. It was my guilty pleasure."

She did her best not to cringe. That was a good eight years ago and while she shouldn't turn her nose up at her start, because those articles did lead her to her first book deal, she often resented the stories the paper made her chase or the spin they required her to put on them. "Wow. I haven't thought about that part of my life in years."

"Your articles made me consider going into forensic medicine," he said. "I think I've got your phone."

"By the sounds of it, I take it you went into a different specialty." She raised her glass and took another healthy sip of her wine. She hated it when anyone touched her cell. It wasn't the personal information she had on the device that she worried someone was tapping into.

It was all the professional shit.

"I'm an emergency room doctor, though I have consulted with the police on a few cases." He groaned. "Crap. It slipped through my hands. But now I think it's under the seat. Hang on." He unbuckled and got on his knees.

"That's cool," she said. "I'm sure you see a lot of strange things on weekends and in the middle of the night."

"Oh, the stories I could tell you." He laughed. "I think I've got it this time." It took him a good three or four minutes to climb back in his seat and hold out her cell.

She took her phone and stared at the screen. "Thanks." It was dark. She tapped it and it immediately asked for her passcode. She sighed. Her paranoia had gotten the better of her.

The plane pitched forward.

Butterflies filled her gut. She'd written six novels about six different serial killers. While she was insanely proud of each novel, something told her that telling Kinley's story would not only be her best work, but changing the perspective of the story would give her readers a more personal experience.

And both her editor and agent had loved the idea so much, they were pulling out all the stops.

Now all she had to do was pull it off.

"By the way, I'm Justin Babcock."

"It's nice to meet you."

"Do you mind if I ask why you're headed to Killeen? Are you doing research for a new book?"

Jolene didn't like to discuss her current work in progress with anyone other than her agent, editor, and the people who were the subject of her material. News outlets always tried to figure out what big crime she was going to write about next, but she wanted to keep the details under wraps, as did her publisher. It wouldn't be until about six to nine months before release date, when pre-orders would go up. However, since her last book was her biggest hit yet, the world was clamoring to find out what notorious killer would be the object of her attention.

That made it even more important for her to keep everything under wraps.

"I'm here visiting my boyfriend." She let the lie roll off her tongue like butter melting over an ear of corn. When Kinley and her husband had told them a friend of theirs would be picking her up at the airport, she'd told them it wasn't necessary. However, Kinley explained it would be the only way she would continue to agree to do the story. And that Cannon Santoro would not only be her tour guide for the week, but that she was to make sure that Cannon was up to speed on all her plans for the week.

She took that more as he was the go-between for her and Kinley since Kinley, while approachable and agreeable to the interview, still had reservations.

Her husband Lefty even more so.

And Jolene understood that. Most of the people she wrote about didn't necessarily want to be the center of her novels.

"Is this a serious relationship or something new?"

Wow. This guy was a bit nosy. She nearly burst out laughing at the thought. She was nosy by nature and if she were interested in what he was doing for whatever reason, she'd be asking the exact same questions.

Though she'd dress them up a little better.

Mentally, she pulled up the picture of Cannon Santoro that Kinley had sent so that Jolene could easily pick him out at the airport, though she knew she'd be able to spot him a mile away. His image would be forever engraved into her mind. She was glad they'd sent her the photograph because she hadn't wanted someone standing in the middle of baggage claim with her name on it for all the world to ponder what the hell she was doing in the middle of Texas. The entertainment channels would start speculating what stories might be connected to this part of the state and it could bring them right to Kinley's door.

That alone would hinder the process.

But Jolene had to consider Kinley's husband and what he did for a living.

"I think that's really not your business, no offense."

"None taken, but that tells me maybe it's more new than serious."

Jolene handed the flight attendant her empty glass and checked her seat belt. She was going to have to put an end to this conversation.

"Are you afraid of flying?"

"Not in particular. I'm just excited that I'm going to be seeing my boyfriend soon." She rubbed her hands on her thighs. Her first meeting with Kinley wasn't until tomorrow at ten in the morning, but Lefty had told her that she'd be given access to

Kinley's personal journals, notes, and other documentation to comb through and that this Cannon fellow would have all of it.

Of course, she got the impression that Cannon would be hovering over her as if she were a toddler playing with knives or something crazy. She understood that Lefty wanted her to treat this story with kid gloves, making sure she respected Kinley's wishes in how she was portrayed. Jolene had no problem with that.

But she did take issue with having a babysitter, especially one as sexy as Cannon, though that could be a distraction she didn't need.

However, if she wanted the story, she'd have to deal with it.

"Are you going to be doing any appearances around town?" Justin asked.

"Not this trip. It's strictly personal."

"Bummer. I would have liked to have purchased a print copy and have it signed by you."

"If you have a business card, I can have my publicist send you one." She almost never gave away books like that to strangers, but this seemed like a good way to pay it forward. Besides, he was an emergency medicine doctor. He might come in handy when she had questions about medical things and maybe this would shut him up.

"You'd do that?"

"Absolutely," she said with a smile.

Her heart beat a little faster as the plane jetted down the runway and lifted up into the air.

It was a short flight to Killeen Fort Hood Regional Airport and all Jolene wanted to do was pull out her laptop and look over her notes. However, not with Mr. Nosy for a neighbor. She suspected being a doctor made him naturally curious and that wasn't a horrible trait.

Actually, she admired anyone who had a healthy interest in others and used the knowledge they gained to do something good for the world.

She hoped she was doing that with her novels.

"That's very kind of you. If you ever need any medical advice, please don't hesitate to look me up."

"I appreciate that."

The plane leveled off and the flight attendant came around with another glass of wine and her latest crime book to sign. Jolene spent ten minutes talking with the nice lady, along with Justin and two other passengers before the pilot came over the loudspeaker, informing them they were coming in for a landing.

The flight attendant took her book and thanked Jolene profusely.

"I feel a bit like a groupie now," Justin said. "Does this happen wherever you go?"

"No," she admitted. "People recognize movie stars and TV personalities, but most don't have a clue what novelists look like, unless you're Steven King. Although social media has changed that some. I think it's just because that last book was so controversial after what happened with the crime family while I was writing it."

"Don't you ever worry about what some of those criminals that you've interviewed over the years might do to you if they ever get mad for whatever reason?"

Of course she did, but she never vocalized it. "Everyone I talk to wants to share their story and they have a say in how it's handled. So, the short answer is no. But I also make sure everyone knows the rules and my publisher's legal team makes them sign all sorts of documents. No one goes into these things lightly."

"I imagine not," he said. "I have to ask. How do you pick what crimes to write about?"

If she had a dollar for every time someone asked her that question, she'd be a lot richer.

She covered her mouth and the slight giggle that came out. All her wildest dreams were coming true and she felt like she was on top of the world. She swallowed the high. It could all come crashing down in one bad review or a major chain not shelving her book.

Or worse.

The readers hating her next story.

"I mean do you pick them or does your editor tell you what to pursue or do the stories find you?" Justin asked.

"My first book was all me, but from there, it's been a collaboration between me and my team."

He leaned in and glanced around. "Do you ever work on active cases?" he asked in a hushed tone.

"Why do you ask?" Most people knew that she never did that. If you combed through her past articles, her podcasts, and the books she'd written, they were all solved crimes.

But his demeanor had her curiosity piqued, so she wanted to know why he'd asked.

"There has been a couple of attacks on women in the area. I've seen two women come into the ER. Neither of them survived. Their injuries were too substantial. I've spoken to the detective heading up the case. He hasn't told me much, but I've been trying to help as much as I can. We believe they are related and are trying to connect them to ones from a few years ago."

"I don't get involved in ongoing investigations." That was a true statement. However, she was aware of more than one serial killer case she'd like to get her hands on. But those were centuries old and there was no way the murderer was still alive to cause her bodily harm.

"You don't ever want to put your investigative reporter instincts to the test?"

"I leave that to the cops. My job is to analyze everything after all is said and done." Not entirely true, but as the ground raced up to reach the airplane's landing gear, it was time to end the conversation. While Justin gave her a nice distraction for the last forty-five minutes, it was time to put her game face on.

She pulled her lip gloss out of her purse and fluffed her hair. Her pulse increased again. Snagging her cell, she pulled up Cannon's contact information and texted him, letting him know they'd landed and we're taxiing to the gate. She quickly stole a glance at the picture Kinley had sent.

Immediately her heart rate picked up speed and

heat spread across her skin as if she'd stepped under a hot shower.

Damn. Cannon put new meaning into the word sexy.

He had these intense dark eyes with a long face and squared chin. She suspected he was in his early thirties, but he had a mature look about him that indicated he'd seen shit.

She knew that look. She'd seen it on the faces of many hardened criminals and cops who'd been around the block a time or two. Military men, especially special forces, always carried a heaviness deep in their soul and it appeared that Cannon was no different.

The lights flashed inside the cabin and the sound of multiple people unclicking their seat belts echoed in her ears.

"It was nice meeting you," she said, deciding it was best to be polite. "I'll make sure my publicist sends you the book." She'd make sure to send that text message as soon as she deboarded the plane. It was important to keep the fans happy and he seemed like the kind of person that would remember not receiving a book when promised.

"Listen. I was thinking maybe while you're in town we could get a drink together or something. I don't have a lot of free time since my schedule at the hospital is intense, but I'd really like to see you again."

"I'm sorry, but I'm going to be really busy with my boyfriend." It wasn't that this doctor wasn't attractive, because he was. But he came on strong and she wasn't interested.

Besides, this was a business trip and she needed to stay focused. And what kind of man continued to ask out a woman when she kept saying she had a boyfriend?

"You have my card if you change your mind." Justin stood, tossing his backpack over his shoulder. "I'm really hoping I hear from you." He smiled and waved.

She did the same.

If she ever needed his help for medical reasons, she'd reach out, but she doubted it would be this trip.

Tapping at her screen, she texted his information to her publicist. She wanted to make sure Justin got his book as soon as possible. That way when she did need to call in a favor, he'd be more inclined to respond.

Now, off to find tall, dark, and handsome.

CHAPTER 3

Cannon leaned against a large post near baggage claim and scanned the group of people heading in his direction. He glanced at his Apple Watch. Jolene had landed fifteen minutes ago and the carousel had spun to life, spitting out the first few bags from her plane.

That had to be a record for the small regional airport. Normally it would take another ten or twenty minutes before anyone could collect their belongings. Of course, it had been a long time since Cannon had flown commercial and even longer since he'd packed anything except his rucksack, which would fit nicely in the overhead compartment.

Or so he imagined.

Jolene had mentioned she would be one of the first people off the plane. He assumed that had been code for first class.

He wondered what that would be like. The last time he'd flown outside of the military, he'd been maybe eighteen years old. He remembered walking past the big plush seats to the main cabin where everyone was packed in like sardines.

Much like being transported in the back of a C-30 en route to a dangerous mission.

Hell, he was lucky if he landed with the plane. Usually, he parachuted out in the middle of the night in an undisclosed location, hoping he was within a half mile of his mark.

A tall woman with long, curly dark hair strutted through the airport. She didn't have those sexy reading glasses on, but she carried herself with a great deal of confidence and that alone was a turn-on. Her heeled boots clanked against the tiled floor in tune with his heartbeat.

His breath caught in his throat.

Jolene's picture didn't do her beauty justice. She had a natural grace that commanded the room. Her style was more down-to-earth than elegant. She had grace and everyone turned and glanced in her direction.

And it wasn't because she was pretty.

That was a given.

It was simply because she was the kind of person people took notice of.

He locked gazes with Jolene and she gave him a little wave with her fingers and a bright smile as if they were old friends. And frankly, it felt like they were. He pushed from the column and strolled in her direction with his heart pounding in his throat. Something akin to adrenaline filled his system.

No woman had ever made his body react this way during a first meeting. Not even a second one.

Or even sex.

Jolene was special and he knew it; he just wasn't sure how to handle it.

He'd stayed up half the night reading her latest book. She had a way with words and he found himself unable to put the novel down.

Somehow, Jolene had captivated him before he'd even met her and that was hard to do.

She glanced over her shoulder and said something to the gentleman walking stride for stride as she made her way toward the baggage claim. Her forehead crinkled. She raised her hand and rubbed the back of her neck, her smile now forced, though nothing short of polite as she continually glanced between the man walking next to her and Cannon.

It didn't appear to be a look of fear, but more of annoyance.

Cannon took that as a sign she wasn't completely comfortable with the man trying to engage her in conversation.

She was supposed to be traveling alone. That was the deal. No assistant or any other associate from her publishing house.

Just Jolene.

So who the fuck was this man chatting her up, acting as if they were best friends? And why did Jolene pick up the pace and make a beeline for Cannon with her arms open?

He swallowed his paranoia. There was no reason to believe that she wasn't enjoying the man's company. Or at the very least, the person was harmless.

Not everyone had an agenda.

And not everyone was a bad person.

"Hey, Jolene," he said as if he'd known her his entire life. "Did you have a nice flight?"

"It wasn't the worst." She pulled him in for a hug. And not just any embrace. She wrapped her arms around him and then planted a kiss right on his lips, letting it linger for a few long moments.

Heat rippled across his skin like a fire out of control. He had to squelch his first impulse, which was to slip his tongue between her sweet, tender lips.

That wouldn't be appropriate.

Not that his embrace was.

"I know this is awkward, but just go with it," she whispered.

"Are you okay?" he asked in a soft voice as he ran a hand up and down her back, letting the hug last for as long as he could. He enjoyed the way she felt pressed against his body a little too much.

"You could have waited in the cell phone lot for me," she said.

"And miss this greeting? Never." He squeezed her hip, keeping his hand on her at all times, playing along, maybe more than he should since he had no idea what the situation was, but whatever. She started it and he wasn't about to end it.

Though what the game was and why, he had no idea. However, he planned on finding out as soon as he got rid of the man giving him the once-over with a glaring eye.

"Aren't you sweet." She looped her arm around

his waist, leaning into his body. "Always the gentleman and spoiling me."

"Do you see your bag?" Cannon asked.

"Not yet," Jolene said. "Hopefully it won't take too long. I'm tired of traveling."

The man dared to curl his fingers around her biceps. That took some balls considering she was currently in another man's arms. "Remember what I said about if you ever need any medical information for your books. I'm just a phone call away."

"Thanks." She nodded. "It was nice meeting you." She didn't bother to introduce him to Cannon. That was a statement all by itself and Cannon wasn't sure what it meant. She could have forgotten the other man's name, or she just didn't want to continue the conversation.

Cannon figured it was the latter.

"The pleasure was all mine." The man dropped his hand to his side. "Hi. I'm Justin Babcock." He looked Cannon directly in the eye. It wasn't an act of aggression, but the way he spread his legs and then folded his arms across his chest, Cannon couldn't help but take it that way.

Cannon let out a long breath. He wasn't in the mood for small talk with a stranger, much less to get into a pissing contest. But his buddy had asked him to keep an eye on Jolene, for a variety of reasons, and if that meant running interference with an overzealous fan, or some dude who had the hots for her, then so be it.

"Oh. Sorry. This is my boyfriend Cannon." She squeezed his arm. "And the reason I'm in town."

He pulled her close to his side and kissed her temple, keeping his lips on her warm skin for a count of six. It was probably over the top but whatever was going on, it had Jolene spooked enough to pretend they were more than friends.

"Oh. There's my bag." She pointed.

"I'll get it for you, babe." He took two steps toward the carousel and snagged the suitcase she pointed at, setting it on its wheels, wondering what the hell she'd packed and if she planned on staying for a month. "We better get going. We've got dinner reservations at that restaurant you love so much." He pressed his hand on the center of her back and gave her a little nudge. "Take care, man." He didn't wait for Justin to respond.

Cannon continued to guide Jolene through the maze of people until they were safely in the parking garage. He glanced over his shoulder and scanned the area, satisfied they hadn't been followed. "What the hell was that all about?" He found his pickup truck and tossed her bag into the bed.

"I sat next to him on the plane. He's a fan, a doctor, and he's got ideas. Lots of ideas."

As he opened the passenger door for her, she rolled her eyes.

"I'd have a private island in the Caribbean if I had a dollar for every Tom, Dick, and Harry that thought they had the perfect crime story for me to tell, but he was especially annoying because he wanted to offer his services."

"As what? A male escort?"

She burst out laughing. "That might have been on his mind as well and he didn't seem to be deterred even when I told him I had a boyfriend." She cringed. "Sorry about that."

"No worries. I'm glad I could drive the point home that you weren't interested."

"But he's an ER doctor with an interest in forensic medicine. I guess he dabbles in it on the side. If he wasn't so interested in me personally, I'd take him up on his expertise, but I feel like I'd be dodging the pickup lines left and right." She narrowed her stare. "I don't have to worry about that with you, do I?"

"You're the one who came on to me with that kiss, so whatever happens, it's all your fault."

"So, you think you're a funny guy."

"Some days." He jogged around the hood of the truck and slipped behind the steering wheel. "Do you have the guy's full name and where he works?"

"Yeah. Why?"

"I want to do a background check." Cannon scanned the area once again as he pulled out of the parking spot and eased through the maze of cars toward the exit.

"That's seriously not necessary. He wouldn't be the first expert who's come on a bit strong."

"It's not just for you," Cannon said. "I have Lefty and Kinley to think about and Lefty would want me to."

"As long as you're not playing knight in shining armor with me. I can't stand that shit."

He paid the parking ticket and headed for the Airbnb that Jolene had rented for the week. It wasn't far from Fort Hood and only about three miles from where Cannon lived, which was nice, though he knew he'd be spending a lot of time in his truck.

Watching.

Waiting.

For what?

He hadn't a clue.

He really didn't know why Kinley and Lefty were so spooked about this interview. The bad guys had been caught and there were no open threats for Kinley to worry about. The only thing was the media and asshole people who didn't understand boundaries.

Of course, the moment the book hit the shelves, they would come out in droves. Lefty and Kinley planned on making a statement long before that happened, cutting the vultures off at the pass. That should placate the media and solve that issue, for the most part.

Until then, it was to be kept under wraps.

"Are you serious? Because you put me in that role when you made me your boyfriend in front of that guy."

"Fair point," she said. "And thank you for going along with it. I didn't want to give him a bigger opening to pursue me."

"I can appreciate that," he said. "Are you hungry? We can stop somewhere and grab a bite if you'd like."

"If you don't mind, I'd rather just stop at a liquor store, grab some wine, and then I'll just order in."

"We can do that too."

"I mean, I prefer to eat alone. I've got a lot of

work to do before the first interview tomorrow and I'm dead dog-tired. But I appreciate the offer."

The oxygen in his lungs flew out like an airplane taking off. The fact she turned down his dinner offer shouldn't affect him one way or the other.

But it did.

And that fucking annoyed him.

So what if she was attractive.

Lots of women were and until recently, he hadn't given serious relationships a second thought.

This last mission had fucked with his head. He wasn't worried about performing his duties in the field. He knew he was ready for that. It was all this contingency planning that his shrink had him thinking about. The what-ifs that he'd always put out of his mind.

Of course, the military had taught him that having a go-to-shit plan was always a good idea.

But this was different. This also had him planning for retirement.

What the fuck?

He was barely past thirty and he figured he'd die doing this.

But then the damn doctor had to go and bring up legacies and family and shit.

"No worries," he said. "Might I suggest ordering

from Cal's Kitchen? They have the best country fried steak and black beans you've ever had."

"Sounds amazing. Thanks."

He pulled into the liquor store parking lot. "Take your time," he said, opting to stay in the vehicle. He took out his cell and found the contact information for his buddy Tate Glavin who worked for the Killeen Police Department. It rang twice before Tate picked up.

"Hey, man, what's up?" Tate asked.

"Same thing, different day." Cannon set the phone back in the cradle and pulled up the information on the doctor. "I need a huge favor."

"Anything. Name it."

"Can you do a quick background check on a Doctor Justin Babcock? He works at Allied Memorial Hospital in the emergency department."

"Why do you want me to do that?"

"He was bothering a friend." Hopefully that would be enough for Tate to say yes. "I don't need a full-on investigation. I just need to know the man is harmless and that I don't have to worry about him harassing my friend." That would be bad enough, but if he came after Kinley, that would be even worse. And that's really why Cannon wanted to check into Justin's background.

Or at least that's the reason he gave himself.

"I'll let you know what I find out."

"Thanks." Cannon spotted Jolene paying for her wine at the counter. "I'll talk to you later." He tapped the red button on his cell.

His next call, after he dropped Jolene off at her rental, would be to Cal's Kitchen. Hopefully they'd deliver to his truck because that's where he'd be for the rest of the evening.

Unless Jolene decided to go out.

God, he hated stakeouts, but he was given strict orders to keep her in his sights at all times.

Unless duty called.

But that wasn't going to happen, so he might as well suck it up and get comfortable.

It was going to be a long night.

CHAPTER 4

Jolene shut the front door of her rental and closed her eyes. With her hand on her midriff, she let out a long sigh. "Holy shit," she whispered. When the good doctor had started to push the idea of them getting together for drinks, she knew she was going to have to put her foot down, and using Cannon as her boyfriend was the first thing she could think of. But the second she locked gazes with Cannon, all she wanted to do was kiss him. She wondered if maybe the boyfriend thing had been some Freudian slip.

She touched her fingers to her lips.

It wasn't meant to be a romantic kiss. Far from it.

But damn, it made her go weak in the knees and the second their mouths molded together, it was like fireworks went off inside her brain.

She fanned herself for a second and then pushed from the door. She had no time for fantasies and even less time for romance. Five other authors had approached Kinley to tell the Alleyway Strangler story and she'd declined each and every one.

But she'd said yes to Jolene because Jolene had promised to tell the story from Kinley's point of view and that was something her editor had gone bonkers over. It wasn't that big of a twist and other true crime novels had gone down the victim road.

However, Kinley was a witness and her boss had been caught up in the whole thing, which set off a chain of events that nearly got Kinley killed.

Her story by itself was unique and Jolene was excited to tell it.

She tugged her suitcase across the small living space and set it in front of one of the bedrooms. When she booked the place, she picked it because it looked newly renovated and it had a big bathtub in the master bedroom.

Stepping into the room, she smiled. It had a big king-sized bed with fluffy pillows. It wasn't a huge room as the bed took up most of the space, but it had a large screen television hanging on the opposite wall and a small dresser. She peeked into the bath-room and her heart fluttered.

The free-standing bathtub was to die for.

She was going to enjoy having a glass of wine while she soaked in that thing.

Taking her cell out of her back pocket, she found Cal's Kitchen and ordered exactly what Cannon recommended. Her mouth watered just looking at the tiny picture on her phone screen. She'd had country fried steak once before and while it wasn't on her diet, she only lived once.

She made her way to the kitchen and put her white wine in the freezer, thankful there was fresh ice in the ice tray. When she got to the liquor store, she'd been bummed that her favorite wine hadn't already been refrigerated because she was in desperate need of another glass. Between what happened on the plane and still feeling Cannon's lips on hers, getting a little buzz on was a moral imperative.

"Cannon," she whispered. What an interesting name. She wondered if it was his given name or a nickname.

Either way, it was sexy as hell.

She found a wineglass and filled it with some ice. She wasn't a wine snob, so cooling it down this way didn't faze her in the least. She poured herself a nice-sized glass and took a sip.

"Oh yeah. That's good." Jesus. She really needed to stop talking to herself. It was habit she picked up when she'd first started writing in high school. When all her friends were out doing teenage things, she was in her room writing about all sorts of different things. If she wasn't sitting in front of her computer, she was pacing and talking to herself.

Her poor parents thought there was something wrong with her and sent her to a therapist who told her mom that Jolene was simply an introvert with a special talent.

From that point on, her parents encouraged her strangeness.

She found her laptop and notebook and set up shop at the kitchen table. She'd been over all this material before. She knew it like she knew the back of her hand, but it couldn't hurt to read it again. As a matter of fact, it might give her a fresh approach.

More importantly, it would get her mind off Cannon.

Her phone vibrated and the screen lit up, letting her know the driver with her food was approaching.

A minute later, the doorbell rang.

When she opened the door, she got more than her food. Her vision was graced with Cannon sitting in his vehicle down the street. He wasn't very well hidden, and maybe he didn't want to be, or perhaps he lived in the neighborhood. That was a possibility since the rental was right around the corner from Fort Hood and Cannon was Delta Force.

"Thanks," she said to the young man who handed her the bag. She gave him a cash tip before setting her food on the end table by the sofa. She really wanted to eat it hot, but she also needed to deal with the man down the street and the sooner the better. She slipped her feet back into her sandals and headed down toward Cannon.

The delivery person stopped at Cannon's truck and handed him a bag.

Wonderful.

She picked up the pace. No way was he going to ruin her dinner. "What do you think you're doing?"

Cannon glanced up and smiled, though a bit sheepishly. "I'm eating dinner and I see you took my recommendation and ordered from the same place."

"Why are you stalking me?" She planted her hands on her hips and glared as she stood on the side of his truck.

"This is not stalking."

"Really? Then what do you call it?"

He glanced in the other direction and rubbed his chin with his thumb and forefinger. "Protection detail?"

"You're not funny. I should call the police."

"But you're not going to," he said with a stern tone. "When Kinley agreed to doing this book, you agreed that someone was going to be glued to your side and that someone is me. I don't want to invade your space, but I'm not going anywhere either."

"Are you planning on sleeping in your truck? Because that's creepy."

"Don't worry about what I'm doing," he said.

She wrapped her arms around her middle. There was no way in hell she'd be able to get a good night's rest knowing he was out here in his truck watching her every move. But what choice did she have?

Invite him in?

Now that would be insane.

Okay. Maybe just for dinner.

"I won't be able to focus on what I'm doing if I'm thinking about what you're doing out here."

"Say that ten times fast."

"You're a regular comedian," she mumbled. She glanced toward the sky. The sun slowly moved toward the horizon. She couldn't believe she was going to do this, but maybe she could take a few lemons and turn them into lemonade. "Grab your grub and come inside."

"Are you inviting me over for dinner?"

She raised her finger. "Just dinner. And then you're going to leave and you're going to make sure that when I look out any window, I don't see you because if I do, I will call the cops." She turned on her heel and marched off toward her house.

She could hear his cowboy boots clicking on the pavement.

"Wait up," he called. "You're practically running."

"I'm hungry and I want my wine. I've been waiting all day for it."

"Do I get a glass?" He appeared at her side, though it was no surprise he'd catch up with those long legs of his. He had a good six inches on her five-foot-seven-inch frame.

"You don't seem like a white wine kind of guy."

"The only alcohol that I don't enjoy is scotch. I've just never developed a taste for it. Outside of that, I'll drink just about anything."

"I suppose I can share one glass with you."

He laughed. "You bought like five bottles."

"I figured I'd buy enough to get me through the

week and I wasn't expecting company." She pushed open the door. "Don't touch my things." She raced to the table, closing down her laptop and shoving her notebook into her bag. She couldn't stand people checking out her scribblings about her work. It didn't matter that he might not understand her madness; she had a method to it and she was also a bit superstitious about it as well. The only people she dared show her work to before it was completed were her agent and editor, and even that made her break out in hives.

"I heard writers were weird about their stuff," he said.

"It's not that. I just don't trust you."

"Then why did you invite me in?" He took the bottle of wine and poured himself a drink. Guess he didn't have a problem making himself at home.

Figures.

He did seem like the cocky type. Then again, she figured most military personnel, especially those in special forces, had to be in order to survive. Their jobs were tough; she knew that from interviewing a couple of Green Berets a few years back.

But they had a sense of humility. She'd only known Cannon for an hour and he seemed like a stand-up guy with a dry sense of humor, which she appreciated.

However, he could be completely full of himself and that would cancel out everything else.

She took her bag of food and pulled out the container, letting the aroma of fried beef fill her nostrils. Her stomach gurgled in anticipation. She took her seat and immediately dug in, doing her best to ignore the man opening his container of food and displaying it on a plate. "I hope you plan on washing that because I'm not going to do it for you."

"I'm happy to," he said. "Would you like me to get you a dish? I'll clean it for you. That way you don't have to eat like a barbarian."

"I prefer it this way." She lifted her fork, full of black beans, and shoved them in her mouth. "It's efficient and not wasteful and I would think a military man would appreciate that. I mean, when you're out in the field, don't you eat dehydrated food right out of the bag?"

He laughed. "But I'm not in some undisclosed location defending my country right now. I'm sitting here with you, enjoying a hot meal and some wine." He raised his glass. "Here's to being civilized."

"Anyone ever tell you that you're weird?"

"My brother every day of my life." He brought the wineglass to his lips and took a slow sip.

She couldn't tear her gaze away and she tried. Hoping her hand didn't shake, she raised her fork and took a bite of her mashed potatoes and gravy. "Oh. That's good."

"I told you Cal's Kitchen was the best."

"That you did." Thank God she was able to lower her vision to her plate, and for the rest of her meal, she planned on keeping her focus anywhere but on the man across the table.

Since when did eating food become sexy?

Normally she found the necessary habit kind of gross. Chewing and teeth showing and chomping sounds were not attractive at all.

Not even close.

Only Cannon was the exception to the rule.

"I have to ask," she said. "Is Cannon your real name or is it some nickname?"

"My real name is Michael, but no one has called me that since I was ten."

She tilted her head. "The military or your team didn't give you that name? Because I thought maybe you were like a bomb tech or an explosive expert."

"My area of expertise is being a sniper," he said.

"Which my brother finds amusing and fits my nickname."

"It sort of does." She brushed her hair behind her shoulders and continued to devour her fried steak. It really was the best she'd ever eaten. It was so good she wished she'd gotten a second helping so she could eat it for breakfast. If she wasn't worried about being judged by Cannon, she'd be ordering it right now. "Maybe subconsciously you became a marksman because of your name."

He waved his fork. "You sound like my ex-girlfriend, who was studying to be a psychologist and she was wrong. From the moment I picked up a gun when I was ten, I was an excellent shot. It was a natural progression."

"Don't you find it ironic that you got your nickname at the same age you learned how to shoot?"

"I hadn't thought about that." He cocked his head. "But I can't help it if my father bought me a rifle for my birthday that year. Or that my uncle took me skeet shooting for the very first time. Or that I joined a local youth riflery team either. So, I don't think any of that is connected to how I got my name."

"Do you like your nickname? Have you ever thought about asking people to start using your real name?" Her writer instincts kicked in, which was a good thing. Focusing on asking him a dozen or so questions kept her mind from mentally undressing him and wondering what his muscles would feel like under her touch.

She had some serious issues right now.

"Why would I go back to Michael when Cannon is so much more interesting?" He pushed his plate aside and topped off his glass. "Besides, no one called me Michael when I was a kid. They all called me Junior and that sucked."

"Was your father's name Michael?"

"No. It was because I looked so much like my brother Tony so they all just called me Tony Junior and then just Junior. I hated it, so when the doctor started calling me Cannon and brother preferred that to Junior and then some people at school started calling me Cannon too, I really pushed it and it eventually stuck." He swirled his wine and smiled. "My turn for a question."

"I might not answer."

"That's your prerogative, but it's a pretty tame question," he said. "What made you want to become a crime writer?"

He was right about it being a benign inquiry, but she didn't always give a truthful answer.

Most people couldn't handle the truth.

But something told her that Cannon might actually appreciate it.

"My parents were murdered when I was seventeen."

He coughed and spit out half his wine.

Her delivery probably could have been a little better. "Sorry. Didn't mean to shock you."

"I expected it to be something close to home, just not that close." He snagged his napkin and wiped up the mess he'd made on his lap. "Where were you when it happened? How did it happen? If you don't mind me asking."

"Normally, I don't talk about it. I changed my name when I was twenty to get away from it."

"Does your publisher know?"

"Yes." She lifted her glass and downed the rest of the wine. It was only her second glass. The one from the plane and this one. So she had no excuse for being loose-lipped. "It came out before I was given my first book contract."

"Now I have to ask. What's your real name?"

"My legal name is Jolene Whittle. But my birth name was Jenny Whitcomb." She shivered. It never failed. Every time she even whispered her given name it gave her goosebumps. It wasn't that she wanted to forget. She never wanted that. But she needed to move on. It was the one case she'd never touch.

Not even if the police ever caught who did it.

He rubbed his chin with his thumb and forefinger. "I'm sorry. But that doesn't ring any bells."

"It might not unless you lived in Virginia."

"I'm very sorry for your loss. That must have been difficult to lose your parents that way."

"It was," she admitted. "I was away at summer camp where I worked as a counselor. It was a month before my eighteenth birthday and six weeks before I was to start college. About the only thing that kept me going was an email my father had sent me the week before telling me how proud he was of me that I stuck to my guns and was following my dreams and that I should never let anyone tell me I couldn't do something." She fought the tears that stung at the corners of her eyes. Why she felt compelled to tell a perfect stranger her life story was beyond her. It wasn't the anniversary of her parents' murders or their birthdays or even their wedding anniversary.

She just missed them.

Plain and simple.

"Sounds like a great dad."

"He was."

"Do you want to tell me what happened?"

She reached across the table, lifted the bottle of wine, and filled her glass all the way to the top. "Only if we take this into the family room where I get the recliner."

"Fair enough." He took the bottle and followed her into the family room where he made himself comfortable on the sofa.

This put some distance between them, which she needed, especially if she was going to get through this story.

Shit. That was it. She hadn't told it since she started the research for Kinley's book and she always rehashed the details of her parents' murders before starting a new novel. It was her way of purging her demons so she could focus on the crimes that were the center of her work in progress. It was the only way she could give them her full attention; otherwise, her parents would seep into the fabric of the novel and that was never good. Normally, she'd go out with her agent and repeat the story to her, but they hadn't time before this trip.

"I feel like I need to qualify why I'm telling you this before I start," she said.

"You don't owe me any explanation. I'm happy to listen for whatever the reason."

"Okay." If that were the case, then she'd use the shit out of him and not worry about giving him clarity into her thought process. "Most of what I know I learned from the detective working the case who was kind enough to share with me all the police reports and to this day, he sends me updates, but it's a cold case and there has been no news in years."

"Wow. That sucks that it's an unsolved case."

She nodded.

"Were there any other victims?"

"Tim, the lead detective, had tied it to two other murders before my folks and seven after, but my parents were different because of my father."

"Why?"

She took a moment to take another sip of wine. Normally, people didn't ask her questions. They would just sit there with their mouths gaping open, eyes wide, with horrified looks on their faces.

"The other victims were women only. No men. You see, my dad was out at his weekly poker game and someone broke into the house. They raped my mom and—"

"Jesus," Cannon muttered. "I can't imagine."

If she was going to get through the story, she needed to keep going. "Sometime between the rape and the murder of my mom, my father came home."

"That's fucking horrible."

"You can say that again," she muttered. "His buddies said he wasn't feeling well and left the game early. I've always wondered if maybe he knew something was wrong with Mom."

"I believe in that kind of shit," Cannon said. "My parents are connected like that. And they have that same connection to me and Tony."

"That's nice."

He nodded. "What does the detective believe happened?"

"He believes my mother was still alive when my dad got home. This is based on the medical examiner's time of death for both my parents, which was only about a half hour difference." She paused to drink more. She didn't want to be drunk, but a little courage never hurt. "And also the other victims of what the media dubbed *The Near-Death Killer*. But in reality, my mother didn't fit the profile."

"Why not?"

"Because all those victims died in the hospital. They wouldn't have made it regardless because of the toxin in their systems and they were beaten so badly."

"How did they get to the hospital?"

"Some of the victims were found in nearby parks

or right in front of the hospital. One was found on a gurney in the hallway. But the key with my mom was the poison. She didn't have that in her system so they couldn't link her with the serial killer."

"But this detective thought differently."

She nodded. "All the rape victims were moved from wherever the crimes were originally perpetrated. There was no reason to believe that my mother would have been any different. And the poison that killed them probably wasn't given to them until right before they were left by the hospital."

"What was the toxin?"

Jolene swallowed her emotions. No one, other than Tim, ever cared this much for the individual details of the cases. Of course, Tim was used to murder and mayhem because he was a homicide detective and it was his job to ask these questions and seek the answers. But even some of her closest friends couldn't even muster up a single question or even a compassionate sentence when it came to this discussion. "Sodium fluoroacetate," she said matter-of-factly. "It can take thirty minutes to kill or a few hours. The thing is they didn't know to look for that until a few victims after my mom, but we know my mother didn't have it in her system."

"So, your father came home and interrupted the killer and ended up a victim himself."

"In a nutshell, yes."

"Were your parents found at home or somewhere else?"

"The cleaning lady found them two days after they were murdered."

Cannon set his glass on the coffee table and slowly stood. He strolled across the room and knelt in front of her, taking her hand. He pressed his lips to her skin.

She swallowed. Hard. She wasn't used to this kind of attention from a stranger. It wasn't that people didn't show her empathy, but they didn't know what to say or how to behave. And she always gave people passes for that because death was hard enough, but murder was an entirely different story.

He tugged her from the recliner and guided her toward the sofa. She should pull away. Not that anyone hadn't ever shown her affection before. People generally gave her a hug after they heard the story, but it was always an awkward one, unless they'd known her well.

She eased onto the couch, allowing his protective arm to stay around her shoulders. She let out a long breath. "I came straight home when I found out. It was utterly horrifying. I could never stay in my parents' house after that."

"I don't blame you."

"Tim worked his ass off to try to connect my parents to The Near-Death Killer. If he could have done that, he could have gotten federal support. There were many similarities with the rape and the torture of my mom." She wiped away the few tears that burned a path down her cheeks. "But without the drugs in her system or the moving of the body and the fact my father was tortured and killed as well, the federal agents wouldn't take it on. Tim ended up having to send it down to the cold case unit and that's where it's been ever since, collecting dust."

"And I take it all these other murders also go unsolved?"

"They do," she said. "But they stopped about five years ago. The cops think either the killer is dead or in jail for something else because serial killers don't just stop and since they had brought the feds in, they have been looking for similar cases in all states. They've even looked into if he possibly changed his MO, which is very rare."

"Did they find anything?"

"There are a few cases around the country that fit

The Near-Death Killer. It's still an ongoing investigation."

"Why haven't you used your skills to look into it?" Cannon asked.

Jolene had been asked that question a million times and again, she wasn't always truthful with her answer. It wasn't anyone's business. But there was something about Cannon that made her want to open up. She couldn't explain it and right now she wasn't going to try. She needed this. "In the beginning, yes. I was like a dog without a bone. I nearly got arrested a couple of times in my quest to find the killer. I became so obsessed that I was put on academic probation my first semester at school. One of my professors sat me down and told me not only was I not helping my parents, or the police, but I was making things worse for myself. He helped me channel my energy on other things and he got me a job at a local newspaper where I started writing about crimes. That's when I decided I wanted to do it for a living, but in a different way because I had very little control back then."

"So why not write a book about your parents? Why not try to force the police to look more closely?"

"The latter I've tried," she admitted as she let her

head fall to Cannon's strong shoulder. "But I don't write about unsolved crimes, especially when we know the killer is still out there doing his thing. And this is too close. I won't do it justice."

"I can understand and respect that." He squeezed her shoulder. "I have some friends in high places. If you'd like, I can ask them if they are willing to take a look at your parents' murders and also check in with the feds. My buddies can find out things that the feds wouldn't dare tell you."

She tilted her head. "Why would you do that?"

"Because Lefty and Kinley trust you enough to let you tell Kinley's story. That says a lot about what they think about your character. But mostly because the case is unsolved and I can't imagine what it would be like to know that a killer was still on the loose."

"There is a part of me that wonders if this psycho is going to come after me."

"I'd say that's a fair fear and good that the name on your books is different, but you haven't answered my question."

"I don't want anyone to go out of their way or put their job on the line for me."

"They won't be," he said. "I'll give them a call in the morning."

"I appreciate it." She pushed from his embrace and tucked her hair behind her ears. "And thank you for listening to me ramble on about this. I don't normally dump on strangers. It's kind of a ritual for me to talk about when I start a new project, but I usually do it with a close friend."

He jumped to his feet. "My ex-girlfriend said about the only thing I was good for in a relationship was listening."

Jolene laughed. "Someday you're going to have to tell me about how badly you suck at them."

"Maybe over breakfast. Cal's Kitchen makes a mean biscuits and gravy." He reached out and yanked her to his chest. "Thanks for sharing your wine with me. You have my number and I'll be right outside if you need me."

"Are you seriously going to spend the night in your truck?"

"I can think of at least a dozen worse places." He kissed her forehead. "Sleep well, Jolene."

She opened her mouth to invite him to stay, but she snapped it shut quickly. That wouldn't be a good idea. She'd been too intimate with him as it was, and she couldn't afford to get too close. "You too." She followed him to the door and watched him casually stroll toward his vehicle.

Damn, he had swagger.

Her cell buzzed.

She ignored it. She didn't feel like talking with anyone.

But five minutes later, it vibrated again, making this horrible noise as it jumped on the kitchen table. She lifted it and groaned.

The good doctor from the airplane.

"Nope. I'm not going to answer it." She tapped the red button, sending it straight to voicemail.

The damn thing buzzed again. This time Justin sent a text.

Justin: *Hey. Sorry to bother you, but I thought you might want to know there was another victim tonight. One of my colleagues at the hospital called me about an hour ago. Her roommate found her and brought her in, but he couldn't save her. She'd lost too much blood. I really think this case is right up your alley."*

No. It wasn't. It was an active case and she didn't do those.

She found Cannon's contact information and set him to her favorites and then turned her phone to privacy. That way, if for some reason Cannon had to reach her, he could. But Justin's calls and texts would go unnoticed.

For now.

She'd respond tomorrow.

She glanced out the window and smiled. She didn't like surprises, and she certainly didn't appreciate having someone glued to her hip, but if she was going to have to deal with it, Cannon wasn't too awful of a babysitter.

CHAPTER 5

Cannon strolled down the street carrying a couple orders of biscuits and gravy and two omelets from Cal's Kitchen. He hadn't the heart to tell Jolene that he lived a few miles away. Or that someone else would be taking the midnight-to-six shift. He probably should have considering all that she'd told him, but he didn't want her worrying about anything. Besides, his buddy had parked in a completely different spot. One that Cannon hoped she wouldn't see.

Thankfully, nothing out of the ordinary happened last night.

He quickly checked his phone.

Nothing from Special Agent Serenity Bale Reddington, his FBI friend. Actually, she was an old

Army friend's wife.

She'd get back to him when she had something. He knew he could count on her for information.

He made his way up the stone path and tapped on the front door.

"Who's there?" Jolene called.

"It's Cannon. With breakfast."

"I'm only letting you in if you've got a mimosa to go with it." She pulled open the door and smiled. "I'm kidding. I have to work and champagne goes right to my head."

"Good. Because I don't do girly drinks."

She burst out with a big giggle. "Somehow I think you're man enough to handle a little mimosa."

"Yeah. You're right."

She stepped aside and let him in.

"Wow. You went home and showered."

"I couldn't come here all smelly. Besides, I only live a few streets away." He set the food bag on the kitchen counter since there was no room on the table. "Actually, just the next neighborhood over."

"I figured this area was all military." She waved her hand toward the sliding glass doors. "Why don't we sit outside?"

"Sounds good to me." He took the bag while she

snagged plates, utensils, and something from the fridge.

She could have turned him away. She didn't have to entertain him, and showing up for breakfast wasn't part of what Lefty had asked him to do. Nope. He was just supposed to keep an eye on her and be there in case Kinley needed anything since Lefty and his team were in the middle of some intense training and he couldn't always be there, whereas Cannon had nothing but time on his hands.

"Did you sleep okay?" he asked.

"Probably better than you." She poured him a tall glass of orange juice. "I love this whole delivery shit. I set this order up last night and it was here by seven this morning."

"So I heard."

She cocked her head. "Heard? What does that mean?"

"Confession time. I didn't sleep in my truck."

"I see. So I had a false sense of security then?"

"No. A buddy of mine was on the lookout."

She narrowed her eyes. "I think I'm insulted." She leaned back in her chair and folded her arms. "I get that Kinley is a bit apprehensive and perhaps even having second thoughts. All of that is normal. But this feels like I'm being treated as a criminal. And I don't like that."

"No. That's not it at all." Cannon didn't want to break Lefty's trust. However, he needed to make Jolene feel comfortable. Cannon needed to find the middle ground and that wasn't going to be easy. "I'm going to be honest with you, but I need you to understand that Lefty is only protecting his wife."

"From me?"

"From the vultures who want to exploit what she went through," he said. "But it's more than that. I don't want you to take this the wrong way. It's just that he's heard you do a lot of behind the scenes digging and he's afraid you're going to stir the pot and possibly upset the wrong people inside the military and that's where I come in."

"To make sure I don't do that," she said with a fair amount of anger lacing her words.

Cannon couldn't blame her for her frustration. He'd be annoyed too if he were in her shoes. "Lefty is still active military, and Delta Force. What we did is highly classified and he can't afford to have people poking around in his life. He supports Kinley and her desire to tell this story, but he doesn't want any backlash. As I'm sure you wouldn't if someone told your parents' or your story."

"That's a fair point." She took the bag of food and started putting things on the plates. "When Kinley and I spoke about how I'd approach this story, she and Gage—or Lefty as you call him—had a long chat with my publisher. Lots of legal documents were signed. I have a lot of boundaries when it comes to the government that I have to comply with and I'm happy to do so. There is nothing to worry about, so you don't have to play bodyguard."

"I'm not going anywhere." He dug into his breakfast. He was going to get fat if he kept eating like this. "Why don't you put me to work. I'm happy to help."

"I don't share my process with anyone except my agent and editor."

Cannon fiddled with his food, pushing it around on his plate while he studied her body language. She was neither closed off, nor open. However, he wouldn't describe her as indifferent either. He did suspect she regretted sharing all that she did about her parents last night. That he could understand. It had been a lot for him to take in and he ended up spending a few hours googling and reading about the double murders.

It had been completely heartbreaking.

"There's got to be something I can do for you."

She nodded. "Stay the hell out of my way." She waved her fork. "And bring me food. This is delicious."

He laughed.

Her cell rang. She pulled it from her back pocket and rolled her eyes before tapping the screen and setting it screen down on the table.

"Something wrong?"

"No. Just someone I don't feel like dealing with right now."

"And who might that be?" he asked.

"Aren't you nosy." She snagged a second biscuit and dunked it in some gravy.

"I can be."

"If you must know, it's that doctor from the plane. He's obsessed with some murders that have been happening and he thinks it would be a good story for me to pursue. I answered him this morning in a text, but he's being quite persistent."

"Perhaps it's not the story he's in hot pursuit of," Cannon said with an arched brow. "Shall we take a selfie and send it to him?"

"I told him I was busy all day with my *boyfriend* and he came back with he wanted to ask me some questions about the murder last night. I guess the woman died in the ER after being treated by a friend of his and this is not the first victim."

"He's right." Cannon took out his own cell and pulled up an article he remembered seeing about a sudden rash of murders. "I believe there have been five or six over the last two years until recently when we've had two just in the past month. Last night's makes three." He held out his cell. "The police have not said serial killer, but there is a reporter that has connected some dots."

"Do you normally follow this kind of thing?" She took his phone in her hands and scanned the article. "If I didn't know better, I'd say you and Justin are ganging up on me."

"Not at all since I've never met the man before yesterday, and I think he comes on too strong." Cannon chose to leave out the fact he had his friend, Tate, run a background check. "But I have a friend with the local police department. He's a detective and he's working the murder cases."

Jolene lifted her gaze. "Has he said anything to you about them?"

"Not really. He doesn't generally discuss his open files with me, but there was one murder that he didn't think was connected, but now he's thinking it might be, and it turns out I knew her."

"A recent one?"

Cannon nodded. "Kaylee Ann Jasper. She was killed about a month ago."

"How well did you know her?"

"She was my ex-girlfriend." Cannon blew out a puff of air. It had been a long time since he and Kaylee Ann were an item. "We broke up about three years ago, but it was a difficult one, for both of us."

"Jesus. I'm sorry."

"Thing is, her case is technically closed. They believe her current boyfriend killed her because they found him two days later with a self-inflicted bullet wound and a suicide note saying he was sorry. That he didn't mean to do it."

"Are you questioning that finding?"

Cannon rubbed his temples. "I didn't at the time, but Tate gave me some information about a girl killed two weeks after Kaylee Ann and it was all just too similar. He's been trying to have Kaylee Ann's case re-opened ever since."

"Oh, my God. All the victims were raped," she said softly. "And beaten. Like my mother."

"I hadn't thought about that," he said. "But sadly that's not uncommon."

"But they were also all moved and not killed at the scene, but left for dead."

"That's true of some, but not of Kaylee Ann. She was found dead on Carl's boat."

"I take it Carl was her boyfriend," Jolene said as a matter of statement and not a question. "And the cops are sure that's where she was raped and killed?"

"That's what they say."

Jolene continued to stare at his phone, tapping at the screen and reading either that article or other ones that came up. Her gaze darted left and right, and she bit down on her lower lip.

"What's wrong?"

"Did you read this?"

"The article is a few weeks old, but yeah, when it came out," he said.

"And you don't see how close this all is to my parents' murders?" She caught his gaze. Tears filled her eyes.

"Can I see my phone, please?" Quickly, he took a closer look at the words on the screen. When Kaylee Ann had died, he'd been out of his mind. He still couldn't believe she was gone. While they never had any chance of getting back together, he still cared about her and wished her well. He didn't like her boyfriend. Not one bit. He thought she could do better than Carl, especially since he'd put his hands on her. "There were no drugs of any kind found in the victims' systems."

"Whoever the killer is knows how to bring his victims close enough to death that there isn't much hope. Last night, the woman had lost too much blood and even if they could have saved her, the trauma to her head would have left her brain dead." Jolene pushed her plate across the table. "For the first few years after my parents' murders, I desperately tried to find other victims. All over the country. I put myself in some pretty bad situations looking for the killer. Once I refocused my attention, I've tried to stay away from my parents' story because I don't want to go down that rabbit hole. It's not healthy for me."

Cannon had felt her passion in her words when he read her book. She cared for the victims and she told their stories with the utmost respect. While he could understand why she didn't want to write about her parents' killer, he struggled with why she didn't want to investigate it. Or have someone else help dig for answers.

Okay. Maybe this Tim guy or whoever was handling the cold case files back in Virginia was keeping her abreast to what was going on, but the second Tate had approached him with the idea that

Carl might not have killed Kaylee Ann, Cannon had started having his own people look into the murder.

So far, nothing had turned up.

"I'm no detective and I don't know anything about this stuff." He set his phone on the table and caught her gaze. "But I do see the connections."

"So, you don't think I'm crazy."

"No. I don't. I have to call my buddy, Tate, for something else. Can I give him the detective's name who handled your folks' murders?"

"I'll text you the contact information and I can give you the cold case team. The woman who heads it up is named Andrea Watson."

"I'll get my people to look into it."

She rubbed her temples. "I'm sorry. This is just too close to home, and I need to collect myself before Kinley gets here."

"Hey. Don't sweat it." He stood and lifted her into his arms and tugged her to his chest. Running his hands up and down her back, he held her close. He wasn't about to let her go.

She let out a guttural sob. "I don't want to cry. I can't do this right now."

"Come on. Let it out. It's okay. You're safe."

"Kinley is going to be here in less than two hours,

and I've got paperwork to go over yet," she said between sobs.

He hugged her tighter, stroking her hair while her shoulders bobbed up and down. He pressed his lips against her temple and let them linger for a long moment. He wished he could take her pain away. He understood grief. While he hadn't loved Kaylee Ann the way she deserved, he still cared about her and wanted her to be happy.

Carl wasn't the man for the task.

But it wasn't Cannon's place to say anything and Kaylee Ann let him know it.

More than once.

Minutes passed as Jolene purged her emotions. He had no problem holding her for as long as she needed.

Only he liked it way too much and he should feel guilty for that. Lefty expected him to keep an eye out for Kinley's best interest.

Not become distracted by the writer.

"I'm so sorry. I don't usually fall apart like this."

"It's okay," he said. "I'd be doing the same thing if I were in your shoes."

She took a step back and brushed the hair from her face. "I highly doubt that."

"No. I think I would. I mean, you've constructed

your life in writing about other people's solved crimes while your parents' go unsolved. You come to Texas to interview someone and find out that there are a few murders that resemble what happened to your parents. I'd say that is absolutely cause for having a slight breakdown. But it's what we do with this information going forward."

"What do you mean by we?" She tilted her head.

"You've got a book to do research for and you've only got a week to do it. Let me look into the murders. That's how I can help you."

"Aren't you supposed to be keeping an eye on me?" she asked.

"I can do both." He smiled. "While you're working with Kinley this afternoon, I'll do some digging, and then we can regroup at dinner."

"While I loved what we had last night, maybe something different?"

"I'll grill." He knew this wasn't quite what Lefty had in mind, but it beat sitting in his truck.

"Thank you. For everything. I don't know how to repay you."

"Just do right by my friends and we can call it even."

CHAPTER 6

Cannon leaned against Tate's unmarked SUV and stared across the street at the emergency room. "Thanks for looking into this for me."

"You know I don't think Carl killed Kaylee Ann, much less killed himself, and that her murder is connected to the Starling and Potter cases. And maybe even the Rubin girl from last night. But there are a lot of surface differences to the cases you gave me this morning."

"You have to admit, though, there are too many similarities not to find it a little creepy."

"There are certainly enough to have a look-see. However, the feds would be all over this if they thought they were connected. This third murder has their attention, but there are still some discrepancies. They need a lot more before they will call this a serial killer."

"What about the murders from last year? And the year before? Aren't they all similar?"

"They are and I've sent them to the feds."

"Send me all the information, okay?"

Tate nodded.

"If Kaylee Ann was part of the mix, do you think the feds would be here? Because that would be four murders in one month."

"That might have made a difference," Tate said. "I'll do some serious digging and asking around, but I'm not going to find anything in a day. You're going to have to be patient."

"I have a call into my FBI agent friend, Serenity. She might be able to help connect the dots."

Tate glared. "Why would you do that? It's only going to bring the heat down on me."

"She's cool and she'll work under the radar until she can't. Her husband and two of her brothers are both Army intelligence working with homeland security. They all like to bend the rules a little."

"If my boss gives me shit, then I can't help you," Tate said.

"I totally understand." Cannon didn't want his buddy to put his job in jeopardy, but he couldn't sit idly by and not help Jolene. Something didn't sit right about these cases and her parents' murders. Maybe it wasn't the same killer, but Cannon wouldn't ever forgive himself if he didn't at least investigate.

"There is a national investigation into The Near-Death Killer; however, the feds really struggle to pull new cases together and they aren't really focusing on it. The last one was about fifteen months ago and it was in Dallas. The problem is there is always a discrepancy for the original rash of killings in Virginia."

"Jolene mentioned that the local cops in Virginia believe the killer was caught on a different charge because the murders stopped."

"That is one theory and these are all unfortunate random killings or some kind of weird copycat," Tate said. "I spent last night finding out as much as I could about The Near-Death Killer and the feds don't agree on a profile."

"That's not good." Cannon didn't know much about profiling, but he did know that when a law enforcement agency didn't have the same opinion about something, nothing would ever get done. "What's the problem?"

"Your friend might be able to give you better

insight, but when we called asking for assistance, they said we didn't meet the criteria for a serial killer, because Kaylee Ann's case is closed as a murder/suicide. I called again this morning based on your hunch about The Near-Death Killer and the agent I spoke to said that they no longer believe all the cases are linked and are currently looking at them from a different angle. They only believe the murders in Virginia are by The Near-Death Killer."

"What do you think?" Cannon believed Tate to be one of the smartest men he'd ever met in his life. His deductive skills were the best in the business, and if anyone could figure out these murders, it was Tate.

"I agree with you. There is something that connects all these murders together and this killer is having fun toying not only with his victims, but with the police. I've seen it before. I mean, it's extremely rare that a serial killer will change his MO, but maybe he's not. In order to understand the MO, you have to understand what's important to the killer and what part of the rituals are crucial and what parts aren't."

"It appears the rape, torture, and slowly dying are all super important to this guy." Cannon ran a hand across the top of his head. He swallowed the bile that smacked the back of his throat. Knowing how

Kaylee Ann had died sickened him. Thinking about her last hour of life filled his heart with rage. He didn't like Carl. Not one bit. But he didn't believe for a single second that Carl had raped and murdered Kaylee Ann.

Cannon might have thought Carl wasn't good enough for her, but that didn't mean Carl didn't love Kaylee Ann.

"But there's something else that may or may not be something that this killer needs."

"What's that?" Cannon asked.

"Of all the cases that I've found or that you've brought me, outside of Jolene's parents and Kaylee Ann, the women died either in the hospital or near the hospital."

Cannon cocked his head. "All of them? How many is that?"

"Nineteen between Virginia, Dallas, and now the three here," Tate said. "But that's only the ones I know about. I wouldn't be surprised if there are more. But there's a catch. Some of them are solved. Or believed to be solved."

"What does that mean?"

"A man was arrested last year and admitted to killing four of the women. He was murdered during transport between the jail and the courthouse."

"How?"

"He was shot. We never found the shooter," Tate said.

"So, that case is unsolved."

Tate nodded.

"I'll have Serenity do some digging. She's pretty high up with the FBI."

"I'd be careful," Tate said. "We don't want to bring attention to this. The last thing we need is the media up my ass, or your friend Jolene's. That wouldn't be good for her current project and it would get you in trouble with Lefty and that's one man I wouldn't want to be on the bad side of."

Cannon laughed. "He's not all that terrifying."

"Dude, you're scary." Tate slapped Cannon on the back. "Not to change the subject or anything, but are you sure you want to go in there? What is it about this doctor guy that has your panties in a wad?"

"He's taken an unhealthy interest in Jolene."

Tate chuckled. "So have you."

"That's the furthest thing from the truth," Cannon said with a heavy dose of irritation. "I'm only doing what a friend asked me to do."

"That's bullshit."

Cannon had known Tate for a long time and he could always count on Tate to be brutally honest.

Sometimes too honest.

"All Lefty asked you to do was keep an eye on Jolene and right now your vision is somewhere else completely. Besides, I told you the man's clean. He doesn't have any kind of record. Not even a parking ticket that I could find. And he's done a lot of good things for the community like volunteering his services at a mobile clinic and he's helped out the cops a time or two as a forensic consultant. The man's a stand-up guy."

"Who is aggressively pursuing Jolene about these victims." Cannon blew out a puff of air. "If he wants to talk about a murder, I'm going to give him the chance to give me his thoughts on Kaylee Ann's."

"You're playing with fire, dude."

"Have you ever known me not to?"

Cannon stepped into the emergency room and immediately had flashes of racing to the helicopter, carrying Skip over his good shoulder while his dislocated one throbbed and ached.

Shots from the enemy still echoed in ears.

Shouts from his teammates telling him to hurry filled his brain.

He sucked in a deep breath and pushed the memories from his mind.

"May I help you?" a young man in scrubs asked.

"I'm looking for a Doctor Justin Babcock. Is he around?"

"I think he's on break. Is there something I can help you with? Are you hurt?"

"No. It's personal. Can you tell him that Jolene's friend is here to see him?"

"Sure." The young man shrugged as he turned on his heel and disappeared through the doors that said Emergency Room Personnel Only.

Cannon made his way toward the vending machine. He pulled out his credit card and got himself a soda. He flipped the tab and took a swig. He seriously needed the caffeine and he figured he'd be waiting for a while.

Only that theory was shot to shit when Justin came barreling through the doors.

"Hey. Is Jolene okay?" Justin asked, not bothering with the standard pleasantries.

"She's great." Cannon put on a wicked smile for good measure. "I was so happy to see her yesterday. It's been too long and this long-distance thing sucks."

"Aren't you in the military? And doesn't that mean you're deployed a lot?"

"That makes it even harder, but we do our best to make it work." Cannon really enjoyed making this man squirm and he shouldn't. His mother would smack him upside the head if she knew how much fun he was having with this.

And God only knew what Jolene would do.

"What brings you here if you or Jolene aren't in need of medical attention?"

"Is there someplace we can go sit and talk? This is kind of personal."

"Okay. Follow me."

Cannon downed the rest of his soda and tossed the can in the recycle bin. He stuffed his hands in his pockets and strolled down the hallway.

Justin led him to a small room that had a sofa, two chairs, a table, and a coffee machine. Justin made himself a cup and waved an empty one.

"No, thanks." Cannon eased into one of the ugly wooden chairs with blue cushions. He swore that every hospital and doctor's office on the planet had the same one. "I really appreciate you taking the time to speak with me. And I'd appreciate it if you didn't say anything to Jolene about it."

"All right." Justin didn't deny that he was trying to

communicate with her, which Cannon thought was interesting all by itself. "What's the problem?" The doctor took a seat across from Cannon. Justin leaned back and sipped his coffee.

"I don't have a problem, but you and I have a common interest. The recent murders." He leaned forward, resting his elbows on his knees. "Besides the fact that Jolene never takes on active cases, we believe one of the victims is my ex-girlfriend."

Justin raised his mug halfway to his mouth before lowering it. His jaw slacked open. "How is that you don't know if she's a victim or not? They've identified all of them."

"My ex is Kaylee Ann Jasper."

"She was murdered by her boyfriend, and he then killed himself," Justin said. "I remember they were at the same party I was the night Kaylee Ann was killed."

Cannon swallowed. Hard.

He hadn't expected that.

"You knew Kaylee Ann and Carl?"

"I knew Carl." Justin set his cup on the table. "But not well. He worked for a pharmaceutical company and I've seen him around the hospital before. I have nothing to do with buying, but my boss does and it was my boss who had the party."

"Who's your boss?"

"Ross Marina. The party was given to celebrate the ER and he invited the pharmaceutical reps, the nurses, doctors, and anyone who services the ER department. He does this every year and it's always a really nice party."

"Did Kaylee Ann and Carl seem like they were a happy couple? Or did you notice anything strange about them that night?" Cannon really wanted to ask if Justin had been questioned by the police, or if anyone from that party had been, but he'd refrain.

For now.

Besides, he'd be able to get that information from Tate.

He hoped.

"I couldn't really say. I didn't really spend any time with them. I said hello to Carl. He introduced me to Kaylee Ann and that was about it. The next day I heard that Kaylee Ann had been raped and murdered and that Carl was missing. I couldn't believe it. Carl might have been an odd guy, but I never pictured him being a killer."

"I have to agree with you on that point," Cannon said.

"I'm sorry about what happened to Kaylee Ann. Is it because she's your ex-girlfriend that you don't want me to tell Jolene that you were here talking to me?"

"Jolene doesn't want me pursuing this because the case is closed. She thinks I'm digging where I don't belong solely because Kaylee Ann was my ex-girlfriend. Jolene has looked at the evidence of these new murders and she doesn't see how these other murders are related. She and I disagree and since Jolene told me you dabble in forensics and have worked with the police, I wanted your opinion."

"I see." Justin glanced toward the ceiling. "I have to be honest; I haven't really thought about Kaylee Ann as being one of the victims of whoever killed these other women. And because I knew Carl and the medical examiner is a friend of mine, I took a peek at the autopsy report. Carl killed himself. There's no question."

"You work with the cops as a consultant, but you're not a forensic doctor?"

"I paused medical school to get a master's degree in forensics. I didn't want to be only a forensics specialist. I wanted to help the living too. So I do both, but more in the ER than with forensics."

"You must not have much time for a social life."

"What doctor does," Justin said with a short laugh. "I still have school loans I'm paying off, though I should be finally done with those next year, and then maybe I'll lighten my load a little bit. Until then, I really love what I do and see no need to change it up. Yet." He went back to sipping his coffee.

"What about the other girls? Do you think they were all killed by the same man?"

"You know I do or you wouldn't be here, but I'm sorry, I can't connect Kaylee Ann to those. I just can't." Justin polished off his coffee and squeezed the paper cup. "Any chance you can talk Jolene into investigating the murders? Because there are others that go back a few years. I've been keeping a file and I know they were all killed by the same person, even the solved ones. But there are just enough inconsistencies that while the police don't disagree with me, it's been difficult for them to get federal help." He leaned forward. "But I also don't think they want it. I mean, no one wants a serial killer in their neighborhood and they want to keep the media out of it."

"You've got a point there. It would create panic."

"That wouldn't be good, but something has to be done," Justin said. "And with three murders in one month, I'd say our killer is escalating. That's never a good sign."

Cannon hated to agree with Justin, but he was

absolutely correct. "There's no way Jolene is going to investigate, but I have some friends in high places. Send me what you have and I'll have my people look into it."

"I don't think I can do that." Justin said. "It's not personal, but I don't know you and I don't trust your motivations. Maybe if you could convince Jolene to work with me on this, then I might reconsider."

Well now. Justin just revealed his true colors.

He wanted a byline.

With Jolene.

Cannon should have seen it right from the very beginning. It made perfect sense.

"I know my girlfriend and she won't ever get involved in an active case." Cannon nearly choked. Not on the fact he used the word *girlfriend* but because it rolled off his tongue so easily and it didn't feel weird.

He told himself it was a simple lie. That he was playing a part and he'd done that many times while in the field. His attraction to Jolene had nothing to do it.

"However, I am going to ask you to do me a favor," Cannon said.

"What's that?"

"Call me when the next victim shows up because

I think together, we can solve this and then maybe Jolene might be interested." Not. But he needed to wet the man's whistle.

"I've got to get back to work." Justin stood, stretching out his arm.

Cannon rose, taking his hand in a firm shake. "It was nice talking to you." Cannon stepped out into the hallway and made a beeline for the parking lot. He wondered how long it would take Justin to text Jolene that he'd come for a little visit.

His cell vibrated in his back pocket.

That answered that question.

He didn't like Justin, but he didn't have a problem using him. Especially if it meant catching a killer.

Now he just had to calm down Jolene.

CHAPTER 7

Jolene shut off her recorder and set her notebook and pen aside. "Wow," she whispered. "That's a lot to take in."

Kinley set her teacup on the coffee table and reached for another cookie. "I haven't told that story in so much detail in a long time. It felt good to do it."

"I appreciate your honesty. I know that couldn't have been easy for you."

"It wasn't. But I'm glad I did it."

"You husband is pacing outside." Jolene pointed toward the front window. "Is he always this overprotective?"

"No. Only when it comes to this. And only because of what we went through. He doesn't like me to have to relive everything and for a while, I didn't want to. After I testified, I just wanted us to live our lives. I didn't want to think about the past. But it's time now. And if me telling my story can help other witnesses and victims testify, then it's well worth it."

"I take it interviewing him is going to be like having a conversation with an angry pit bull."

Kinley laughed. It was a sweet sound. Calm and fun at the same time. "No. He'll open up to you. He's got other things on his mind besides this."

"Like what?"

Kinley tilted her head and pursed her lips.

"Sorry," Jolene said. "My career makes me overly inquisitive."

"No worries. But since I'm in here and Gage is out there, do you mind if I ask you a few things?"

"Not at all, but I have one more question." Jolene wasn't going to give her a chance to say no. "Why does everyone else call him Lefty but you call him by his given name? And what should I call him?"

"He'll always be Gage to me. Lefty, to me, is his Army name. And his buddies will always call him that. But I can't. He's my Gage. You can call him Lefty. He'd probably prefer that."

"Good to know."

"Now it's my turn." Kinley shifted in her seat.

"And I wouldn't even bring this up except for the fact there was another murder last night and it's one of the things that is weighing heavily on Gage's mind."

A brick dropped to the pit of Jolene's gut. This was not the discussion she expected. She opened her mouth, but she had no idea what to say.

"About a month ago," Kinley continued. "Cannon's ex-girlfriend—"

"I know about Kaylee Ann's murder and her boyfriend's suicide."

"Then you know that Cannon doesn't believe that Carl killed himself after murdering Kaylee Ann."

"He's mentioned that to me," Jolene admitted. "What happened between Kaylee Ann and Cannon?"

"Delta Force was more important to Cannon than her, and she dumped him and he didn't seem to care that much. It broke her heart and he's felt guilty about that. He cared about her, but he wasn't in love with her and they weren't meant to be together. But Cannon is a good man. The best. And he's not going to rest until he finds out what really happened to Kaylee Ann. Or Carl for that matter." Kinley carried herself with a sense of style and grace that most women never developed. She wasn't pretentious by any means, nor did she act as if she thought she was better than anyone else. She was simply elegant. "Is he trying to elicit your help?"

"No," Jolene admitted. However, she wasn't sure if she should tell Kinley about the text the ER doctor had sent or not. Jolene would for sure confront Cannon about it later, especially since he hadn't responded to her text. She didn't like that he went to Justin behind her back and brought up the murders.

Or that it appeared he asked for his help.

Or that Cannon was investigating the killings on his own.

She couldn't afford to be dragged into the spotlight.

But what if they were connected to her parents? What if somehow The Near-Death Killer had made his way down to Killeen, Texas, and he'd made that his new stomping ground?

Had Jolene just opened the door to the past?

"Cannon knows I won't get involved with an ongoing case, but there's a doctor that wants me to look into it as well. I'm not really sure why, except maybe this ER doctor is looking to make a name for himself. Or he's hitting on me or both. But Cannon just went to him about these cases and asked the doctor not to tell me."

"And I take it the doctor didn't listen to Cannon," Kinley said as more of a statement than a question.

"Nope. I got a text about an hour ago from the doctor telling me that he got a visit from Cannon who was asking questions about these murders, including his ex-girlfriend."

"I can't speak for why the good doctor chose to reach out to you, but perhaps there is something else you should know about Cannon that might help you understand why he did that and why this is so important to him."

"What's that?"

"What I'm about to tell you I'd appreciate if you kept to yourself. I'm only giving you the information because I promised Gage that I'd let him put eyes on you during our time together, so Cannon isn't going anywhere." Kinley leaned forward. "Right before Kaylee Ann was murdered and Cannon came home on medical leave, he and his team were involved in a mission that went sideways. I don't know the details. That's classified. But Cannon's buddy saved his life and the lives of his teammates. Unfortunately, the man who did that will never be the same and can't ever go back in the field. Cannon blames himself. And we think he somehow blames himself for Kaylee Ann's death."

"I know that feeling," Jolene said with a heavy sigh. "Why would he believe he's responsible for his ex-girlfriend's murder?"

"He has this weird idea that if he could have loved her, she wouldn't have ended up with Carl. Now, you can't tell Cannon I told you this, but on more than one occasion, Carl hit Kaylee Ann."

"Shit. He can't take that on himself."

"But he does. And even though he doesn't believe Carl killed her, he wished he could have loved her like she deserved. He thinks if he had, she'd still be alive."

"None of that is his fault, but even if his head knows that, his heart will always tell him something else and that's a tough place to be. He needs to change that narrative or he's going to be in a dark place forever." She rubbed the back of her neck. Intellectually, she knew that if she'd been home and not away at summer camp that didn't mean her parents wouldn't have been murdered. Playing the what-if game was a dangerous one and always made her question her decisions.

Which wasn't a good thing.

This was why she didn't like looking into open cases, or her parents' murders.

But she couldn't ignore what was happening right in front of her face. Not this time.

"When Kaylee Ann was first murdered, he accepted the police report. It wasn't until another girl turned up dead and his buddy Tate thought it looked too similar and that got Cannon's wheels spinning."

"I'm sure this ER doctor hasn't helped." Jolene pinched the bridge of her nose. She never told anyone she interviewed about her true identity. Some figured it out and questioned her or the publisher. Most everyone was understanding. They knew she'd approach their stories with respect and honesty, especially considering what she'd gone through.

But if they didn't know about her past, why tell them.

However, this was an entirely different situation.

"I think I should tell you something that I don't usually tell those I'm writing about."

"If it's about your parents, I already know," Kinley said. "When you approached me about doing this book, I was more than skeptical. I've been approached by a good five or six other authors. All excellent writers with decent reputations. I'm sure they would have written excellent books. But I wasn't much interested in telling my story, until you approached me."

"Why?"

"Your writing voice touched me. Not only do you have a way with words, but your compassion reached deep inside my soul. I read all your books and dug into your podcasts. You seek truth more than justice. You look to uncover peace and not revenge. I felt as though when you tell a story its more about understanding the people involved, and not the crime itself, and that was something I could get on board with. However, it was when I found out what happened to your parents and that the case was still unsolved that I realized you put all of your emotions into your work. I can more than relate to that. So can my husband, his team, and Cannon."

"I appreciate you saying that."

"It's the truth." Kinley glanced out the window. "It's getting late and I can see that Cannon has returned. Gage said he has about a two-hour window he can give you tomorrow. When do you want me to come back?"

"How about after lunch? That will give me enough time to digest anything that your husband says and I can go over my notes from today."

"Sounds good." Kinley stood, smoothing down her slacks. "I'm sorry for your loss."

"Thank you." Jolene walked her to the front door. "And thanks for the insight into Cannon. He's been very kind to me since I landed."

"I'm not surprised." Kinley smiled. "Cannon has a big heart, but he doesn't give it freely. I have a feeling you're the same way."

"I don't know what you're getting at." Jolene's heart skipped a beat.

"I think you do." Kinley tugged opened the door. "I'll see you tomorrow."

Jolene squinted as the sun hit her eyes. She nodded at Cannon who was in deep conversation with Lefty.

Cannon held up his finger, indicating he'd be with her in a minute.

She'd take the time to use the little girls' room and freshen up. And perhaps get a drink.

She could certainly use one.

Jolene leaned against the fence and watched Cannon as he flipped the steaks. They hadn't said much to each other since he'd gotten back and that had been almost an hour ago. He opted to borrow her shower and change his clothes before he started on dinner.

Now he sipped his beer and stared off into space while she savored her wine.

It had been a long day and she really should spend some time typing up more notes. However, she had a million questions.

And she needed a few answers.

Only she had no idea where to start and that was an uncomfortable place for her to be.

He glanced over his shoulder. "I feel like you're either tossing daggers at me or trying to size me up."

"It's a little bit of both," she admitted. "I don't understand why you'd go to see Justin. He said you were quite aggressive."

"Did he now." Cannon laughed. "That's not a fair assessment at all. What else did he have to say about our little chat?"

"That you told him to back off and to leave me alone. That I was your girlfriend and that he should stop giving me topics for research or offering to help."

"You've got to be kidding me. I didn't once mention that I knew the two of you were having any conversations. I actually went there under the pretense that I wanted his help."

"He did say you were pretty upset over your ex-girlfriend and were certain she was killed by someone other than her boyfriend and that you wanted his help to prove it." She shook her head. "He thought I should know that he believed you were still hung up on her."

"Not really how that went down and you know that's not true." Cannon placed the sizzling steaks on a couple of plates and pulled the corn off the grill. "But since he believes the other murders are connected, I wanted his take on Kaylee Ann and Carl's so-called murder/suicide. I have to say that for the most part, Justin is professional in his opinions, at least when he was speaking to me. But something doesn't sit right with me, especially if he's going to blatantly lie to you. Even if it's to make one of us jealous because he's trying to get into your pants."

"That was crude."

"Sorry, but we both know it's true." He sat down and pushed his shades on top of his head and sliced into his meat. "I told him if he shared his theories and findings with me, I'd give them to my friends in high places. He basically told me no, but if you were involved, he might reconsider." He lowered his gaze. "Have you heard from him in the last hour or so?"

"I haven't checked my phone since you returned, and I don't plan on it. Last I left it with him was that I was just here to spend time with my boyfriend, who if he wanted to seek answers about his ex's death, he was free to do so." She shook her head. "Justin came back with *don't you think your boyfriend is a little obsessed with his ex-girlfriend?* I didn't respond."

"This is why I'm a little concerned about this guy, but since Tate says they have used him in cases like these, I want to pick his brain."

"I'd rather be kept out of it."

"I'll do my best," he said. "Can I ask you a question about your parents' deaths?"

"Sure," she said. It wasn't often that she felt so comfortable with someone that she responded so quickly, but she had nothing to hide when it came to Cannon. At least not when it came to this.

"Did the killer take anything from your house? I ask because the necklace that Kaylee Ann always wore went missing when she died. It was kept from the media. Tate told me that things were missing from some of the murder victims, but it doesn't appear to be a trophy kind of thing because it's so random."

"Did he tell you what kind of items?"

"No. He didn't and I didn't pry. But I might now." He leaned back and held her gaze, waiting patiently for her answer.

She took a bite of steak and slowly chewed.

This piece of information was kept from the press too, and she's never told a single person. Not one. There were only three other people who knew and that was Tim, Andrea, and an FBI agent.

"My mother had this cross-stitch pillow on their bed that had their names and wedding date on it. I've never been able to find it and my dad's computer went missing."

"That last one is a big-ticket item. What did your dad do for a living?"

"He was an attorney and professor. Oddly enough, he taught criminal law."

Cannon's cell rang. He pulled it from his pocket. "It's Serenity."

"Who's that?"

"A friend of mine from the FBI."

"You called them?" Suddenly her appetite disappeared. She tossed her napkin to the plate. "Why the hell would you do that? I told you I don't want to investigate my parents'—"

"You're not. I am." He pushed his chair back and crossed his legs, tapping the screen on his cell, putting the call on speaker. "Hey, Serenity. How the hell are you? How's Cove? The kids?"

"Cove is great. He and Ledger are outside playing with the offspring as we speak. So, before it's bath and book time, let's get down to business."

"Sounds good to me," Cannon said. "What do you have for me?"

"A whole lot and a little nothing." Serenity had a dry sense of humor. She had to when she'd been the only girl in a male-dominated family that were all Army. "First, the only official cases of The Near-Death Killer we have are those in Virginia, two random ones in Delaware, and one in Baltimore, all around the same time."

"I've never heard about those cases," Jolene said.

"Who's that?" Serenity asked.

"Jolene Whittle." Cannon pushed the cell closer to the middle of the table. "The crime writer."

"I know who she is, do you?" Serenity asked.

"He knows my true identity. Tell me about those other cases."

"They were linked a few months after your parents' case was closed," Serenity said. "But we didn't want it leaked to the press."

"What about the cases in Dallas or down here in Killeen?" Cannon asked.

"Those have been harder to make the connection, though not for lack of trying. But the murder victims in Texas didn't have any drugs in their systems. More than half died in the hospital due to complications from their injuries. Where most of the ones up north died before they got to the hospital."

"That could be the killer perfecting his crimes," Jolene said.

"It very well could be, but the killer took something from the murder victims in the north. A trophy of sorts. Not in the south. Not that we can tell."

"Except for Kaylee Ann," Cannon muttered.

"We've been over this a million times," Serenity said. "I've looked at the ballistics. Unless someone held Carl's hand to his head and helped him pull the trigger, he killed himself."

"Maybe," Cannon said. "But I still can't believe he killed Kaylee Ann."

"You once told me that he hit her and if that's true, he could have easily killed her." Cannon lowered his gaze. He sucked in a deep breath and rubbed his temples. "He might have been a douchebag, but he wasn't a murderer."

"I can't believe you're defending him." Jolene stood. "A man who will put his hands on a woman in anger will absolutely go off the rails. Now if you will excuse me, I need a shower." She stormed off into the kitchen, closing the sliding glass doors. Once inside, she found her cell and checked the messages.

Eight from Justin.

Fucking wonderful.

She was about to put her cell in her purse when a phrase caught her attention.

Another victim. She's not dead. I'm treating her as we speak, but it doesn't look good.

Jolene dropped her cell. She raced toward the patio, running right into the glass door. She yanked it open. "Cannon. We have to go. Now."

"Where? Why?"

"The hospital. There's been another attack. I can't let this go. I know what I said about not in—"

"Serenity, I'll call you back." He snagged his phone. "Let's go."

"Do you really think this could be connected to my parents?" she asked.

"One hundred percent."

CHAPTER 8

Cannon laced his fingers through Jolene's and tugged her through the emergency room doors. "Did Justin respond to your text?"

She raised her hand, which held her cell. "He says she's in critical condition." She tilted her head. "He's not hopeful."

"Did you tell him I was coming with you?"

"I didn't see the need," she said. "While I appreciate Justin letting me know about this latest victim, I wouldn't even be in the know had he not dragged me into this mess. I'm not thrilled that I find myself diving down this rabbit hole when I should be focusing on my book."

"I can call one of my buddies to take you home if you'd rather."

"No. I'm staying with you. As much as you annoy me sometimes, you're the lesser of all evils."

"At least you said all." He laughed. "Where did he tell you he'd meet you?"

"He said there was some sort of lounge if we went through those doors and down the hallway—"

"I know where it is. I spoke to him there earlier." Cannon scanned the waiting room. Tate had mentioned he might be at the hospital, but if was, he was somewhere else. "My cop friend said the woman stumbled into the ER."

"That's horrible. Did he say anything else?"

"Yeah. And I'm not sure how I feel about this information, but Justin wasn't on duty when she came in."

"Seriously?"

He continued to take long strides. His heart pounded in his chest. His stomach sloshed as if it were filled with rough seas. "According to Tate, Justin had left the ER. His shift had been over for an hour, but he'd been doing paperwork, and then he'd gone for a walk. When he found out what happened, he came back in to help. One of the nurses told Tate he's like that. Always wanting to help."

"You say that with some disdain."

He pressed his hand on the small of her back as

they entered the small room. "I know why he doesn't trust me. He's jealous. But I can't figure out why I have such a hard time with him."

"Could it be the same reason?" She plopped down on one of the chairs and crossed her ankles. "God, that sounded way too conceited. I'm sorry."

"No. It's a legit observation." He peeked his head back out in the corridor, making sure no one was around. "I'd be lying if I said I wasn't attracted to you and that if you were going to be in town for more than a week, I'd certainly consider asking you out."

"So, you are jealous."

"It's not that because I have no reason to be. And I'm not that guy. I like you." He shrugged. "I have no problem admitting that. But if you don't return those feelings, there isn't anything I can do about it. Jealousy doesn't do me any good and it isn't going to get me the girl. In this case you."

She smiled. "In a weird way, that's the sweetest thing anyone has ever said to me."

"I'm glad you think so." He chuckled as he leaned against the doorjamb so he could keep a watchful eye out. "There is always some randomness to life. There can be one or two coincidences. Like him sitting next to you on the plane. Unless he'd been stalking you for months, I'd buy that." He turned.

"Did he say where he was coming from or what he'd been doing?"

"No. And I didn't think to ask. To be honest, I was trying to be kind, but also sort of blowing him off. He does come on strong."

"Have you gotten any weird emails? Text messages? Or fan mail in the last few months?"

"I get a lot of that shit," she admitted. "I have a team of people who go through that so I don't have to deal with it. I couldn't tell you about any of it."

He ran a hand across the top of his head. "Would you mind putting me in touch with them?"

"Sure, but what are you thinking?"

Cannon's head pounded. His mind was fractured with two different trains of thought. One about the murderer and one about the good doctor.

And neither one was good.

"You're not going to like it."

"Probably not," she said. "But I want to hear it."

"I can't shake the feeling he's been watching you and waiting for the right time to approach you about his theories."

"That's crazy. Why would he do that?"

"For his fifteen minutes of fame? Or because he's obsessed with you and thinks this is the way to your heart. There are any number of reasons. But there's something I neglected to tell you."

"I don't like secrets."

"I know and I'm sorry. I didn't keep this from you on purpose. I just wasn't sure how to process it." He rubbed his jaw. "Justin knew my ex and her boyfriend."

"What?" Jolene shot to her feet. "How?"

"He barely knew them, but I don't like how Justin is connected to all of these murders and how he's pursuing you. It makes the hair on the back of my neck stand on end." Cannon saw Justin turn the corner, heading in their direction. "We'll have to finish this conversation later. He's coming."

"Wonderful," she muttered. "I didn't particularly care for him, but I didn't think he was that big of a whack job."

Neither did Cannon. He figured he wanted to get into Jolene's pants or maybe work with her, or both.

Now Cannon wondered if it bordered on an obsession and if this started before she boarded that plane.

And that made the wheels in his brain spin harder and faster and he didn't like the road his mind was taking him down.

Justin stepped into the room and gave Cannon

the once-over. He turned his attention to Jolene. "I wasn't sure if you were going to come and I have to be honest, I was hoping you weren't going to bring your boyfriend."

"Where she goes, I go." Cannon hadn't meant to puff out his chest, but Justin had drawn a battle line and Cannon didn't understand why. It was over the top and Jolene had made it clear she wasn't interested in Justin that way. She'd gone out of her way to pretend to be with Cannon.

That said a lot.

So what the hell did Justin really want?

"Jolene, I really need to talk with you. Alone."

"What is this about?" Jolene pushed herself to a standing position and took three steps. She wrapped her arm around Cannon's middle. "Whatever it is, you can say it in front of Cannon. We have no secrets from each other. So if it's about my work, he knows everything."

"But do you know everything about him?"

"What the hell is that supposed to mean?" Cannon asked.

"The woman that we're trying to save had a piece of paper with your name written on it," Justin said. "I'm surprised the police haven't picked you up for questioning yet."

"What's the victim's name?" Cannon asked with a thick lump in his throat. He took Jolene's hand and squeezed.

"I can't tell you that." Justin glanced over his shoulder. "The nurse that helped the victim to a wheelchair as she stumbled into the ER said she whispered what sounded like Cannon's name and she thought she said you'd done this to her."

"That's impossible," Jolene said.

Cannon appreciated the vote of confidence, and while the statement was true—there was no way he could have done such a horrible thing—there were gaps in his day where he was completely alone and no one could vouch for his whereabouts.

That was a problem.

And it was his word against a nurse. Two honorable people in trustworthy professions saying two different things. The nurse would be going on hearsay from a near-dead woman who was carrying a piece of paper with Cannon's name.

The question was where did she get it and why?

It was reasonable to consider she was in such bad shape that she didn't write that herself. So who did and again, why?

"This is why I chose to stay and help with this

patient. If we can save her, she can tell us who did this to her," Justin said.

What a fucking conceited statement. Cannon felt sorry for the ER doctor who was on the clock when the lady in question had arrived. Nothing worse than being told your skills aren't good enough and you need to be micromanaged.

Justin glanced at his watch. "I don't have much time. Jolene, can I have a word with you alone?"

"No," she said sternly.

Justin planted his hands on his hips. "Please don't make me say this in front of him."

"Him is not going anywhere." He looped a protective arm around her shoulders. "So whatever it is you want to say, just say it."

"I don't know what she's told you about her past and what happened to—"

Jolene held up her hand. "What the hell do you know about my life?"

"I told you on the plane. I used to listen to your podcast when I was in medical school. I followed your career and anyone who has done that would know who you really are, but I didn't know if he did."

"Don't talk about me as if I'm not in the room. And

I'm her boyfriend. Of course I know her true identity. But what the fuck business is it of yours?" The last thing Cannon needed was to deal with a stalker.

"It's not," Justin said. "However, I have a master's degree in forensics and I often consult with the police."

"Do you know Tate Glaven?"

"The detective? Yeah. I've met him a few times. He's working on these last few murders. Why?"

"He's a buddy of mine," Cannon said. "Now what did you want to say to Jolene that has to do with her past?"

"The first two murders I hadn't put any of it together. But this last one made me go back and google your parents' deaths," Justin said. "I think we're dealing with the same killer."

Jolene pinched Cannon's hip.

Hard.

He winced.

"Have you voiced your suspicions to Tate?" Cannon pulled her closer, running his hand up and down her back. This wasn't news to either of them, but hearing it from Justin had to have been difficult.

"Not yet," Justin said. "I wanted to talk with Jolene first. I felt I owed it to her."

"The first call should have been to Tate." Cannon

let out a long breath. "But what I want to know is how is it that you know so much about her parents' deaths? I mean, I find it weird that you do. I didn't until we started dating. Why would you go look it up?"

"Are you serious?" Justin laughed.

"Dead. You're an ER doctor. Not an investigator."

"I'm also a forensic specialist. I work with police regularly on cases just like this." He leaned forward. "My opinion is valued and once I saw this woman, I knew. I just don't know why she was carrying around your name clutched in her hand."

The sound of boots hitting the tiled floor echoed in Cannon's ears. He stuck his head out the door and smiled as Tate practically ran down the corridor.

"Hey, man," Tate said. "How are you?"

"Not so great, you?" Cannon said.

"I've had better days." He glanced around, nodding at the doctor, and then turned his attention toward Jolene. "It's good to see you again." He leaned in and kissed her cheek.

"You too," she said, playing along as if she'd known him, which it would have been suspicious if she hadn't known one of her boyfriend's childhood friends.

"Okay. So, let me fill you in on some things I'm

sure Justin hasn't told you because he can't due to patient/doctor stuff. But I can," Tate said. "The victim is Leslie Stoller."

"Jesus. No. Please tell me this is some kind of twisted, cruel joke." His eyes welled with tears. He turned, tugging Jolene with him, wrapping both arms around her body. He rested his chin on the top of her head.

"I'm sorry, Cannon. But it's Leslie." Tate reached out and squeezed his forearm.

"Now it makes sense why she'd have a piece of paper with my name on it." Cannon kissed Jolene's temple.

"Who is Leslie to you?" Justin asked.

"My high school sweetheart." Cannon sucked in a deep breath. "She got married about five years ago and she has a two-year-old little boy." He took Jolene by the shoulders and took a step back before turning his attention to Justin. "You should have called me the second you saw that note with my name on it." He poked Justin in the center of his chest. "I want to see it. You hear me?"

"Relax," Tate said. "I've got it in an evidence bag. However, Justin, you didn't clue me in on that juicy piece of information right away. I had to learn about it from one of your colleagues. Why?"

Justin raised his palms to the ceiling and dropped his hands to his sides, slapping them to his thighs. "Because I found out the two of you are friends and I thought that would taint the investigation."

"Oh. But you had no problem telling me that she had that note in her hands," Cannon said. "And you made it sound like the cops were looking at me as a suspect at first even though you all along thought it could be the same killer as the person who murdered my girlfriend's parents." He clenched his fists and then released his fingers, wiggling them. He had half a mind to punch this asshole right in the nose, but it wouldn't solve anything except perhaps get Cannon kicked out of the hospital.

"I'm doing what I think is best for my patient and I'm trying to help out a friend." He tilted his head. "Jolene, I really do have your best interest at heart and I do think this is the same killer. We should really—"

"There is no 'we,'" Jolene spoke up with a terse tone. "I've tried to be gentle and kind from the very start. I've even had my publicist send you a couple of signed books already with a personal note, which I didn't have to do, but I have no desire to work with you, investigate with you, or discuss my parents' murders with you. So, please stop texting me, calling me, or communicating with me in any way. And if this is the same killer, then I want the police to handle it, and Cannon can speak on my behalf. Do I make myself clear?" She laced her fingers through Cannon's and squeezed so hard he thought his hand was turning white.

"I was only trying to help," Justin said.

"Thanks, but no thanks." Jolene caught Cannon's gaze. "Can we go home now?"

"Tate?" Cannon asked.

"Go. I can catch the two of you at your house."

Cannon guided her out of the room and toward the north exit so they didn't have to go through the emergency room. "I'm moving you into my house."

"Is that really necessary?"

"Yes. I don't trust Justin. He might not have a record and he might be squeaky clean, but I believe he's been stalking you for some time."

"You mean like before the airplane?"

"Unfortunately, yes. So I can't trust that he wouldn't know where you're staying. But he doesn't know where I live and I have a state-of-the-art security system."

"What about this killer?"

"And that's the other reason I want you at my place. This is all connected and until we've figured it out and this murderer is behind bars, you're glued to my hip."

"I can think of worse things to be attached to."

He paused, taking her chin with his thumb and forefinger. "That's the nicest thing anyone has ever said to me." He brushed his lips over her mouth in a slow, tender kiss. She tasted like honey on warm sourdough bread. He groaned. "You're a dangerous woman."

"I'll take that as a compliment." She smiled.

It was going to be impossible to keep his hands to himself.

"Interesting place." Jolene set her bag on the table next to the sofa. She glanced around the family room. It was scantily decorated, but what he did have screamed all male between the dark-colored leather couch and the poker-playing dogs hanging over the top.

"Until I picked you up at the airport, I was a bachelor." He curled his fingers around her biceps and stared into her eyes. "How are you holding up?"

"I'm exhausted to tell you the truth." She leaned into his strong frame, wrapping her arms around his shoulders. She had no idea why she trusted this man and not just to protect her life. "I still don't understand how me moving here will make a difference. If anything, it makes Justin question if we're together or not."

"There's a reason I left my truck in the driveway and two friends of mine are going to stay there. It will look as though we're at the house. If he's got eyes on it, we'll know soon enough, and me and my buddies can make a move."

She dropped her head to his chest and let out a long sigh. He'd explained all that when they snuck out the back door of her rental. In theory it made sense. "Do you really think Justin is dangerous?"

"I believe he's gone to a lot of trouble to get your attention. If your chance encounter with him on the airplane wasn't a random meeting, then we have bigger problems and that's on top of dealing with this serial killer."

She tilted her head. "Is there any chance I can take a look at the victims' files?"

He palmed her cheeks. "I've asked Tate for them and he's going to get me what he can."

"What about Kaylee Ann's and Carl's?"

"I have all those, plus Tate's notes. Why?"

"I shouldn't have kept this from you, but the killer tried to make it look like my dad killed himself."

Cannon cocked his head. "Tried? Why wasn't he successful?"

"A couple of things. My father didn't speak English well and he wrote it even worse. His suicide note was partially in German and he left clues, though nothing that helped the police catch the killer."

"What else?"

"He supposedly used his right hand, which is impossible and not because he's left-handed, but because he'd been in an accident and he couldn't even hold a glass of orange juice, much less raise a gun and shoot himself with it."

"Was there a residue test done on his hand?"

"It was positive, but all the experts agreed that he couldn't have pulled the trigger without help."

Cannon kissed her forehead. "Carl definitely had his fingers on that trigger when it went off, but there were also signs of a struggle. However, the medical examiner's report indicated it could have happened during the fight with Kaylee Ann and considering he had hit her before, it's actually possible."

Jolene reached up and touched the side of his face. She studied his kind expression and adoring eyes. There was something soulful about the way he reached inside her and touched her heart. It felt as though she'd known him her entire life. "And yet you don't believe a man who was known for beating women could have killed her."

"I know he didn't." He took Jolene's hand and kissed it. Her skin sizzled. "He was a lot of not-so-great things and I wanted her to leave him. Not because I wanted to be with her. I wasn't any good for her either, though not for the same reasons."

"Why are you so sure he didn't do it?"

"At first I thought he had done it, but Tate came to me with some new information about the other crimes and he thought the medical examiner was too quick to rule Carl's death a suicide. He's been trying to get it re-opened ever since."

"Has he told you much about that?"

"No. I'm a sniper. I shoot things. I don't solve them."

She forced herself from the comfort of his embrace. "Killers will change their MO to accommodate new circumstances. That's what my dad was to The Near-Death Killer and maybe that's what Carl was too." She pulled out her tablet with her private notes.

The ones she never showed anyone.

The ones she wished she could forget about, but they lurked in the background, haunting her dreams.

She'd stopped researching and hunting for her parents' killer years ago; however, she couldn't let it go no matter how hard she tried.

She typed in her passcode and pulled up her notes. "Do you remember the cold case cop I told you about, Andrea?"

"Yes. Tate's got a call in to her and he said he'd let me know what he finds out."

"I'll send her a note to give him all that we've gathered," she said, holding up her hand when Cannon opened his mouth. "Andrea's had a few murders come across her desk that she thought might have been early murders by The Near-Death Killer that didn't go quite as planned. She has a theory that the killer could be a cop or a first responder."

"Why?"

"After my parents were murdered, the killer got smarter and better."

"Tate told me that happens a lot."

"It does," she admitted. "But the killer started leaving messages for the police about previous murders. And things only the police knew or the people who'd worked the crime scene. It was one of those things kept from the media."

"With good reason." He took the tablet and

scanned the information on the screen and then set it on the coffee table. "It's late. We can look at all of this with fresh eyes in the morning." He lifted her bag off the sofa. "I'll take you to your room."

She hadn't the energy to argue. All her thoughts had started to muddle together. He was right. It was time to take a break and let things settle.

Twiddling her hair, she followed through the kitchen to the back of the house and down a hallway.

"It's only a two-bedroom and we'll have to share a bathroom."

"I'm sure we'll manage."

He strolled into one room and set her bag on a queen-sized bed with a dark-blue quilt and two pillows in white cases. There was not a single wall hanging. In the corner was a small desk with a computer screen and a printer. "There are clean towels in the bathroom and I'm in the room across the hall if you need anything."

"Thank you. For everything."

"You're welcome." He leaned in and brushed his mouth over her lips.

She wanted to grab ahold of him and never let go, but he pulled away before she mustered up the courage.

"Good night," he whispered.

She closed the door and leaned against it, staring up at the ceiling. A memory of her parents filled her mind. "I can't let it go this time. I'm going to find your killer."

* * *

Cannon wrapped the towel around his waist and stepped from the bathroom into the hallway. Jolene's door was closed, but the light was still on. He hesitated for a long moment, but decided it would be a bad idea to disturb her now.

Besides, he needed to do a few more things before he called it a night.

He sat on the corner of his bed and pulled up Tate's number.

It rang once.

"I told you I'd call you when I had more," Tate said.

"You know I'm not very patient." Cannon rubbed the back of his neck. "Did you get all the information I sent you?"

"I did and I also literally just got off the phone with that cold case cop, Andrea. She had a lot of interesting things to say and we're both on the same page."

"What do you make of this Doctor Babcock guy? I had Jolene call her agent and editor to look at all her fan letters to see if there's anything that might indicate Justin had been trying to reach her."

"That's a good idea," Tate said. "I've learned a few things about him that are disturbing."

"Like what?"

"I'm going to start with the local stuff," Tate said. "Justin has been helpful in other cases when it comes to forensics. He can be bothersome and I personally don't like him poking around my shit. However, the medical examiner, Kurt, says he's a great asset, but the ME's assistant, Cheryl, had a little different story."

"Oh, yeah? And what's that?"

"Cheryl thinks Justin is creepy, to use her words. And she's caught him more than once in the ME's office, poking around. Cheryl said the ME always defends him, but she's suspicious. She doesn't understand why an ER doctor is always wrapped up in some of these forensic cases or why Kurt is always consulting with him, and I have to agree, especially with what this Andrea from Virginia told me."

Cannon's heart rate went up by ten beats a

minute. "Why do I get the feeling I'm really not going to like this."

"Because you're a smart man," Tate said. He cleared his throat. "Andrea informed me that there was a resident emergency doctor named Justin Babcock that was on duty when two of The Near-Death Killer victims were brought into the hospital."

"In Virginia? After Jolene's parents were murdered?" The hair on the back of Cannon's neck stood on end.

"I know. It creates more questions than answers and why didn't he say anything?"

"Especially when he told Jolene he knew who she really was. He's obsessed with her and this case."

"You don't have to sell me on that. The only question is what kind of danger is he and for that, I need to know his true motivations," Tate said.

"Did Andrea have any insight?"

"Some. As did Cheryl. They both believe that Justin has an unhealthy need to be a hero. Cheryl gave me some names of nurses and residents to talk with. They paint a picture of an egotistical doctor who likes to save the day. Only, he couldn't in the cases of these murders."

"That's a little suspicious."

"I agree, but don't go thinking he's some deranged killer," Tate said.

"That's exactly where my mind went. And Cheryl had an edge to her voice. Something else is going on there, but I haven't figured that out yet. Have you looked to see if he's ever worked in Dallas?"

"He hasn't. He went from Virginia to here. I'm working on finding out what brought him to our fine town. I've got a few other names I need to contact, and Serenity is doing some digging for us. I need you to keep your eyes open and take care of Jolene."

"That I can do." He set his phone to the side and rubbed his temple.

The door squeaked open.

He jumped to his feet, snagging his weapon from the desk, aiming for the opening.

"It's just me," Jolene said, holding up her hands.

"Jesus. Next time let me know you're coming." He set his gun down and adjusted his towel before it fell to the floor. "Are you okay?" He tried not to let his gaze lower, but he found it impossible since all she wore was a tank top, with no bra, and boy shorts that hugged her body a little too closely.

He bet if she turned around, her cheeks would be hanging out.

He blinked.

"I don't want to be alone," she whispered.

"Come here." He pulled her into his arms, running his hands up and down her back. Her skin felt like a flowing stream of warm water. "I'd rather you not be by yourself either."

She laughed. "I almost invited you in the night you slept in your truck."

"I didn't actually sleep there." He kissed her sweet lips. It was like someone had dipped them in sugar. Everything about her made him feel like he was alive and had purpose again.

And that utterly terrified him in ways he hadn't expected.

Yet, he welcomed the sensation.

He lifted her flimsy shirt up over her head and tossed it to the side. He cupped her breasts and fanned his thumbs over her hard, tight nipples.

She hissed, digging her fingernails into his shoulders.

The way her body responded to his tender touch had been nothing he'd ever experienced. He knew how to please a woman and he was confident that he'd be able to push her over the edge and he'd enjoy doing it. However, no lady had ever made him question the importance of his own pleasure.

And right now, his didn't matter.

Not one single bit.

The only thing that mattered was making sure that Jolene understood that in this moment, she was the center of his affection.

Gently, he pushed to the bed, lifting her legs and tugging her shorts to her ankles, tossing them to the floor. He rested her feet on his shoulders and glided his fingers and tongue into her, enjoying her soft moans. He focused only on her body, taking his cues from the way she responded.

When her muscles tightened and her stomach quivered, he stood, removing his towel.

She wrapped her legs around his waist. "Yes. Now," she whispered, lifting her hips to him.

He didn't hesitate. He gave her want she wanted. He'd always give her what she asked for and he'd never stop.

Never.

The intense emotions swirling around in his mind, his gut, and his heart were nothing like he'd ever felt before. His brother told him falling in love was like getting the wind knocked out of you. When it happened, there was no stopping it and it came at you like a runaway train.

And when you least expected it.

Cannon had never believed in love at first sight.

But as she called out his name in the throes of passion, he knew he'd be forever hers. Even if she didn't want him or love him, there was no denying she'd stolen his heart and he'd never be able to get it back.

His orgasm tore through his body like an exploding volcano, the hot lava coating his skin from his head to his toes, only it didn't burn. Not in the way to hurt him, though he'd never be the same again.

She clutched his shoulders, trying to catch her breath.

Rolling to his side, he pulled the covers over their bodies and held her close. He had no intention of letting her go.

Ever.

Only that was an insane thought. He was Delta Force and she lived in Virginia.

Resting her head on his shoulder, she kissed his chest. "For the record, this would have happened even if all this weirdness hadn't happened."

"I have to admit, I thought about it the second I laid eyes on you at the airport," he said.

"Yeah. Me too." She tilted her head. "But neither of us really do relationships, do we?"

"It's not that I don't want one. But my job is not only dangerous, but it keeps me away for long period of times."

"It's also who you are," she said. "And my career puts me in a room for months, alone, where I forget to eat, change my clothes, even shower sometimes."

"That's gross."

She laughed. "I'm sure I'd still smell better than you after a mission."

"Without a doubt." He pressed his lips against her temple. "So, where does that leave us?"

"Enjoying the moment for as long as we can."

Jolene stepped outside onto Cannon's back patio and brought her mug to her lips. The steam from her coffee hit her nose. The bitter scent awakened her senses. She took a long slow sip and stared at the sun. While she'd slept better than she had in years, she still had strange dreams about her parents. Her therapist had told her it was how her mind processed the unsolved portion of their deaths and the fact that Jolene couldn't do a deep dive into finding out why.

It wasn't healthy for her.

Only, now it would be devastating for her not to investigate the connections between the murders in Killeen and her parents.

Especially the similarities to Cannon's ex-girlfriend.

She shivered.

"There you are." Cannon's voice coated her eardrums like hot fudge drizzled on cold ice cream. "I'm sorry that Lefty had to cancel on you this morning."

"He has a good reason. I mean he can't tell the United States Army he doesn't feel like working today."

Cannon wrapped his arms around her middle and she leaned back into his strong chest. The intense connection she had to him frightened her not only because it came out of nowhere, but because she didn't know much about his life. She believed he was a good man. One of the best.

But she'd never been this trusting of another human this quickly before. It was in her nature to question everything. In her world, everyone had a motive. No one did something for another person just to be nice. There was always a reason, and it wasn't necessarily one pure of heart.

That didn't make that person a bad person. Far from it. It simply meant they needed something and were willing to do whatever it took to get it.

It was human nature.

"Besides, he should be done early and will swing by around three and I'll do an interview with the two of them together."

"What time is Kinley coming?"

"Not until eleven, so that gives me plenty of time to go over the material that I should have last night instead of playing kissy-face with you." She turned and set her mug on the table. Resting her hands on his shoulders, she gazed into his cool-blue eyes. It was like staring into a warm embrace. "And talk through some of these cases down here that might be the same killer."

"Let's sit down." He pulled out one of the patio chairs and waved his hands.

She swallowed. "You've learned something while I took my shower, didn't you?"

"I had a phone call with my friend Serenity, and Tate found a few interesting things from the ME's office that Cheryl sent over along with a disturbing report from the chief of staff at the hospital." He took a seat across from her and clasped his hands together, leaving them on top of the table.

"This doesn't sound good." She took another desperately needed sip of her morning's lifeblood. She couldn't function well without at least two cups of coffee and preferably some bacon, but she wouldn't go asking for Cannon to find some and whip it up for her. There was an app for that.

"It gets worse," Cannon said. "Justin was in medical school when your parents died. He'd already gotten his master's in forensics and was working part-time in the morgue. His name is on some of the paperwork."

She lowered the mug and harshly set it on the table. Some of the hot liquid sloshed over the rim and hit her skin, stinging a tad. "Are you serious?"

"Unfortunately, I am. To add insult to injury, he was a resident and worked in the ER when some of the victims died."

"Jesus," she muttered.

"Justin was also on the plane with you starting in Virginia. He upgraded his ticket to first class on the second leg to sit next to you."

"How the hell do you know that?" she asked with a narrow stare. A bad taste bubbled up from her gut and not even a good gurgling with mouthwash was going to get rid of it.

"I know people in high places and I called in a few favors."

She wasn't sure how she felt about how invasive Cannon and his people could be, or how easily he could find out information about Justin, or anyone for that matter. On the other hand, if it kept her safe and helped solved some murders, she had to be all for it.

"But seriously, how do you know he upgraded to sit next to me?"

"He told the airline ticket agent that his girlfriend was on the flight and he'd splurged for her and decided he wanted to splurge for himself too."

"I don't know what's scarier. That you can find that shit out or that he was that desperate to sit next to me." She ran her fingers through her wet hair. When she got to the ends, she twisted them. "Do we know how long he was in Virginia? Or what he was doing… Oh shit." Her heart dropped to the bottom of her gut.

"What is it?"

"I had a big book signing the week before where I did a reading. I hate doing those things."

"Where was it and what is your definition of big?"

"It was held in a hotel convention center. It was a multi-author event. I wasn't the main attraction. But the place was packed. Probably three hundred people or more. I ran out of books, which I don't normally do, so that part was great."

"You don't remember seeing him there?"

She closed her eyes for a long moment, trying to recall as much of the long afternoon as she could. There was the one mother-daughter duo she remembered because the young girl had been attacked and beaten and her father had lost his life saving her. It was a heartbreaking story.

The killer had been caught, but still, the pain in that girl's eyes still haunted Jolene.

There were a couple other fans that stuck out either because they were victims or they were law enforcement or just plain weird.

But she hadn't seen Justin.

She blinked. "I think I would have remembered him. I mean, he comes on strong."

"He does. And that's another thing that bothers me. The chief of staff has three complaints about his behavior at work."

"What exactly does that mean?" Her pulse increased.

"Justin filed a formal complaint regarding another doctor, but only after his colleague went to the chief of staff with an issue regarding a patient."

"Please don't tell me it was one of the murder victims."

Cannon ran a hand over his unshaven face. "Two victims."

"What happened to the other doctor?"

"She's been suspended while there's an internal investigation into what happened. To try to paraphrase what Tate told me, there is question on whether or not the other doctor gave proper care and that's why Justin stepped in. The other doctor states Justin shoved her out of the way and within the hour both victims were dead." Cannon blew out a puff of air. "The truly frightening part of this doctor's statement is that with last night, with Leslie—"

"Justin wasn't on duty," Jolene finished Cannon's sentence for him. "So this doctor was just suspended yesterday?"

"Nope. About an hour ago. Justin filed the complaint last night. But once again, this gets worse," Cannon said. "Justin had similar problems at the hospital in Virginia. Before it could escalate, he moved, and I've heard he's got feelers out for a job as a head ER doctor."

Jolene's mind filled with a hundred questions but only one answer and she sure as hell didn't like it. Her hands shook. "Are you thinking what I'm thinking?"

"It's the only thing that makes sense."

She stood, strolled to the end of the property

line, and hugged her middle. "This is insane. There is no way I was sitting next to my parents' killer on a plane or that he's the same man who's killing these women down here or who killed your ex. It can't be." She rubbed her temples. Talk about information overload. "There are too many disconnects. No one could possibly pull all this together and make it stick." She turned. "I've been writing and investigating true crime for too long not to see all the problems with this."

"I know. I might not know anything about this stuff, but I can see what a stretch it is. However, when you lay out all the pieces of the puzzle, it makes sense."

"After my parents died, I went down this horrible rabbit hole trying to find their killer. I became so obsessed I didn't even recognize myself. It's why I never look into active unsolved cases. When I do that, I can't stop until the killer is caught and brought to justice. My heart won't allow it."

"I can understand that." Cannon stood and pushed the chairs under the table. "I'm going to go talk with Cheryl from the ME's department and do a little more digging. Tate doesn't have enough to bring Justin in yet, so that's my highest priority."

"I can't sit here and do nothing." She took five

long strides toward the house. "I've got to do something."

"I need you to go through everything you have and then all the information dump that Tate and all my sources have found on every other case that might be related. You're the only one that might be able to connect it all." Cannon took her chin with his thumb and forefinger. "Tate will have a guy in an unmarked car outside the house at all times and the men on my team will be taking turns checking on you. I want you to do your work with Kinley. Lefty said she's real excited to be working with you, especially when she had her reservations about doing the book to begin with."

"It's going to be hard to concentrate. I'd rather be out there with you," she said.

"Trust me. I want to nail this bastard just as badly as you do." He brushed his lips across hers in a tender, loving kiss.

She wanted to fight these fierce emotions. She wanted to believe they were pure lust and infatuation.

But her heart knew differently.

And her soul demanded to let him in.

"I better get going." He ran his thumb across her cheek. "You text or call me if you need me. I'll pick up no matter what I'm doing. If I can't for some reason, you'll get a text. If you don't, you call one of the men on this list." He pulled out a piece of paper.

"Now you're scaring me."

"I don't play by the same rules as my buddy Tate or my friends at the FBI. Nor do my buddies in Delta Force, and if I go dark, it's because we're taking matters into our hands and doing it our way."

"I don't like the sound of that." She palmed his cheek. "I don't want anything to happen to you. I'd never forgive myself."

"I'm not going to do anything stupid like take the guy out, but I'm not going to let him get away with murder either."

She wrapped her arms around Cannon. "Just come back to me. I want this to last a lot longer than a moment."

"So do I."

CHAPTER 11

Cannon strolled into the diner. He pushed his sunglasses up on the top of his head and glanced around until he found the woman he was looking for. He felt guilty for not being completely honest with Jolene about some of his findings. He wanted to read the reports before he sent them. This new evidence could be especially painful. To find out that some of the victims had sodium fluoroacetate in their system, but their toxicology reports were altered during the autopsy. It made him wonder if the same had happened to her parents.

Cheryl sat in the far back corner booth of the greasy spoon. She fiddled nervously with the straw sticking out of her water with a lemon wedge. Her eyes grew wide when she caught his gaze.

"I'm Cannon," he said as he slipped into the bench. "Thank you for taking the time to meet with me."

She set a large envelope on the table and pushed it toward Cannon. "I could lose my job over this." She leaned to the side and stared at the door. "Or maybe get killed."

"Tate has someone looking out for you." He glanced over his shoulder before taking it and setting it on the bench. "If things go as planned, the ME's office will be subpoenaed for this information within days anyway."

"Doesn't matter. I'm also breaking the chain of evidence. My boss will have my head."

"And do you think your boss is doing something illegal?"

Cheryl laughed. "That's what I don't understand. If what Tate believes is true, why the hell would Kurt help a murderer? What's in it for him?"

"That depends on what motivates Kurt. If Justin has something on him and is blackmailing him, it could be all about saving his career and reputation. Or it could be about money."

"Could Kurt be the killer?"

That was an interesting question and one that they'd asked themselves. But Kurt had never lived in

Virginia. "I know Tate is looking into all possibilities, but we both know Justin is the best suspect and what you handed me is why." He rested his hand on the envelope. "I have to ask. How did you end up with the original medical examiner reports on the victims and not just the ones that Kurt changed? But also the forensic reports that Justin altered." Every single unsolved case that Tate had that resembled The Near-Death Killer had either Kurt's signature on the ME report or Justin was the attending physician.

Or both.

It was a small town and a small hospital.

It wasn't unheard of to have that happen.

But to have Justin associated with so many cases in Virginia, that was a huge red flag.

The only ones that didn't have his name attached to them were the ones in Dallas, but Serenity found out there had been a forensic convention that week and Justin had attended.

Go figure.

"And why didn't you give them to Tate sooner?"

"You don't have all the murders. I've been suspicious for a few years, ever since the first time Kurt came to me and said he'd made a mistake and had to refile an autopsy. He asked me for the old one to shred. I told him I'd take care of it for him, no problem. He got pretty annoyed and told me that it was the kind of fuck up that he'd get in trouble for. I told him I had his back, and that wasn't good enough. He got pretty angry and I gave him the report. After that, I tried to make copies of all autopsies of murder victims. I hadn't made the connection to Justin until the murder-suicide of about a month ago."

Cannon swallowed the tightness in his throat. Cheryl had no way of knowing she was talking about his ex-girlfriend. "What helped you make that leap?"

"The toxicology report was changed. In the original they found sodium fluoroacetate. In the one that was filed, they found nothing. Also, in Carl's, the one filed said he was high as a kite on cocaine. But the original one said he was clean. Now you tell me which one is true?"

"Neither one of them died in the hospital, so how does Justin play a role in this?"

"He's observed or participated in both autopsies."

"Well, shit. That's a big revelation." Cannon took the envelope in his hands. "Thank you for getting this to me."

"Just get the bastard. Women in this town are tired of living in fear."

He nodded. "There is an unmarked car in the parking lot. It's dark blue. The man sitting in it has a mustache. He's going to follow you so don't be worried. If anyone else follows you, call 9-1-1 and then call this number." He pushed a card with Huck's cell toward her. "This is one of my team members. If you get spooked, day or night. He's close by."

"Thanks."

Cannon patted her hand. "It's going to be okay." He stood, tucking the envelope under his arm.

It was time to put an end to Justin Babcock and his killing spree.

* * *

Jolene paced in Cannon's family room. Every three or four minutes, she stopped to peek out the front window. She glanced at her cell. Kinley was only ten minutes late and that wasn't a big deal.

So, why was she so nervous?

Maybe it's because she'd spent the better part of the morning going over case files that she knew without a doubt were the work of The Near-Death Killer and she also knew that murderer had killed her parents.

But she'd never be able to prove it.

She wiggled her fingers and made her way toward the kitchen to get a glass of water. What she really wanted was a stiff drink, but it was way too early for that.

Ding dong.

She jumped.

Shit.

Rolling her neck, she made a beeline for the front of the house. She needed to focus on anything other than her parents' murderer. She pulled open the front door and gasped. A cement brick hit the pit of her stomach as if it fell from a twenty-story building and landed in the basement in four seconds flat.

"Sorry to startle you," Justin said as he pushed his way into the house.

"Get out." She shoved back, but to no avail.

"Now, now. Is that any way to treat an old friend?"

"I can't even call you an acquaintance," she said behind a clenched jaw. She knew she shouldn't bait him, but she couldn't keep her mouth shut. "What the hell are you doing here?" Her pulse kicked up a notch. If he was standing at the front door, either the police officer assigned to watch her had stepped away or something bad had happened to him.

She figured it was the latter. "How did you know where I was?"

"When you dropped your cell on the plane, I had found it within seconds of your dropping it, so it was still unlocked. When I was on the floor, pretending to find it under the seats, I made sure you shared your location with me and I've been tracking you. Interesting that you changed location. I have to wonder about you and your boyfriend. But I'm kind of over it now."

She swallowed the bile that smacked the back of her throat. "Why are you here?" She planted her hands on her hips. Her cell was in her back pocket. She needed to get to it and find a way to reach Cannon.

Or one of his buddies.

Or 9-1-1.

"I thought it would be a good idea for us to sit down and chat." He glanced around. "Without your boyfriend."

"He'll be home soon and he won't like you being here, and we have nothing to say to each other, so I'd appreciate it if you left." She pulled out her phone. "Or I'm calling the police."

He quickly snagged it from her hands. "No, you

won't." He shook his head. "I thought you were smarter than that."

"What do you want from me?"

"I wanted you to write our story." He took her by the arm and shoved her to the sofa. He pulled a weapon from his back.

This shit got a little too real. She curled her knees to her chest and wrapped her arms around them. Her heart beat so fast she thought it might pound right out of her chest.

"But now someone else is going to have to do it." He sat on the corner of the coffee table with the gun on his thigh and his finger on the trigger. "And I'm going to have to kill you. It's horribly ironic, don't you think?"

"You're not going to get away with this."

"But I am," Justin said. "I've been getting away with it since I was seventeen years old."

Her jaw slacked open. Her chest tightened. She couldn't tell if her heart rate sped up or slowed to a dangerous pace. She'd gone over all her notes about The Near-Death Killer and the cases she'd found hadn't gone back that far. Of course, she'd been young and her investigative skills back then weren't as honed as they are now. Then again, that's one of the reasons she didn't do open cases. It wasn't her job to catch the killer. She focused on being the voice for the victims and the ripple effect these killers had on the lives they ruined.

"Does that shock you?" he asked with a wicked grin.

"Not really," she said as she put her feet on the ground. She needed to get her bearings. Justin might have done something horrible to the cop sitting outside the house, but he couldn't have taken out Cannon and his entire team. He would be here soon and he would save the day.

All she had to do was keep this asshole talking.

And if her instincts were correct, Justin liked the sound of his own voice.

"Whatever gave you the idea that I would write your story? You'd have to have been caught for that to happen."

"Well, to be honest, I didn't want you to write about me, the good doctor, who tries to save people. I wanted you to write about the killer that the cops couldn't catch. The one that got away. The one that haunted you."

"I'm not haunted by you. I don't lose any more sleep over the lives that you've taken versus other serial killers."

He lifted his weapon and placed the cold metal

on her bare leg. "But I murdered your parents and I made it so they could never link it to me."

"You tried to make it look like a murder-suicide and you failed."

He laughed. "I've learned from that mistake. But still. Because there were no drugs found in your mother's system and her death was different from the others, it's not my kill."

A cold chill shot up Jolene's spine. Her stomach sloshed about as if she were being tossed about at sea. He had no regard for human life. "Did you change my mother's toxicology report as well?"

He nodded. "Your father came home just after I injected her with the drug. Otherwise, I wouldn't have given it to her. But I got lucky that I was working in the morgue then and I swapped out some reports. From then on out, I made some changes to my process." He rubbed his gun up and down her leg. "However, listening to your little podcasts, I wanted to get your attention. I wanted you to talk about how you thought there was a connection, like you'd done early on, but you stopped. I can't tell you how disappointing that had been."

She vomited a little in her mouth. "You've been watching me all these years? Waiting?"

"I can be a patient man. But imagine my surprise when I overheard you talking with your publicist about your upcoming trip to Killeen. I couldn't believe it. I bribed a few people to find out when your flight was and I made sure I was on it."

"And what was your plan?"

"To get you to see that your parents' killer was escalating and that only you could do something, but I hadn't anticipated that you were coming here to be with a guy, but I don't understand why you were staying somewhere else at first."

"He had problems with the air-conditioning and neither one of us like to be hot."

"I don't really buy that, but it doesn't matter. He was a problem I had to take care of."

She stiffened her spine. "What did you do to him?"

"Nothing yet. But he's not going to live to see tomorrow."

"What the hell happened?" Cannon jumped from his truck, taking his communications system. He adjusted his weapon on his hip. "Are you okay?"

"I'll live." Detective Drew Barron sat in the back of an ambulance one street over from Cannon's house. He'd taken a bullet in the shoulder and a knife in the gut. "Your unfriendly doctor snuck up on me when I was doing my perimeter check. He shot me first and then stabbed me when I was down. I played dead and called it in."

"Smart move." Cannon ran a hand across the top of his head.

"Tate's talking with your buddy Huck. Justin is inside." Drew groaned and the EMT wrapped up one of his wounds. "They are in the family room. So far, just talking."

"We've got to get him to the hospital," the EMT said.

"Thanks." Cannon jogged toward where Huck and Tate were huddled in the corner two houses down. His cell buzzed in his pocket. He pulled it out.

"Hey, Lefty. Did you hear what happened?"

"Yeah. I'm five minutes out. I've got Oz with me. Tell your cop friend we've got this. We don't want to spook this guy with a SWAT team."

"I'm on it. I'll see you soon." He tapped his cell and shoved it in his pocket. "Talk to me, Tate." He took the binoculars that Huck handed him and inhaled sharply. Nothing worse than seeing the woman you were falling for, hard, with a gun pressed against her thigh by some asshole. "Tell me you've got more than this to take him down?"

"Oh. We do," Tate said. "He was blackmailing the medical examiner."

"With what?" Cannon asked.

"Kurt has a pill problem and Justin has been holding that over his head. Only, Kurt was too scared he was going to lose his job to look into what Justin wanted to change. And too stoned all the time. But when his wife threatened to leave him two weeks ago, he decided to clean up his act. The second I started questioning him, he didn't think twice about blowing Justin in. He's at the station giving his statement and working out a deal so he doesn't see the inside of a jail cell, but sadly, he'll never practice forensic medicine again."

"At least he's doing the right thing," Huck said. "I think one of us needs to be at the front of the house in case they go on the move."

"Agreed." Cannon pushed his earpiece in. "Oz and Lefty are on the way. Stay in touch."

Huck tapped his ear. "You know I will. Let me know the plan when you've got one." Huck disappeared around the side of the house between the bushes and the stucco.

"The new guy seems good."

"He's the best," Cannon admitted. "It's going to be a pleasure working with him." He pointed toward the road. "Here comes Lefty and Oz. You're going to have to stand down for this one."

"I had to call in the gunshot wound to my superiors. They think I'm on the hunt for the perp. So you don't have much time."

"Once we're in place, extraction shouldn't take very long."

"Just don't kill Justin. I'd like to take him in alive," Tate said.

"I won't make any such promise, especially if he keeps waving that gun at my girlfriend."

Tate tilted his head. "Are you tossing that word around for real now?"

"If she'll have me and we can figure out this long-distance shit, absolutely."

* * *

Jolene shivered. She'd had a million nightmares about what it might be like to have a gun pointed at her, but she had no idea what the hard, cold metal would feel like against her skin.

It was worse than anything she could imagine.

"What is your plan any—" Before she could finish her sentence, her phone rang, startling her, making her jump.

He raised the weapon and pointed it directly at her face.

She swallowed.

He snagged her cell from the coffee table and held it up for her to see.

Cannon.

She let out a yelp.

"Answer it," Justin said. "Put it on speaker, but if you say anything about me being here or warn him, I'll kill you right now."

She nodded.

"Tell him everything is fine. Tell him you made some connections, but you can't talk about it over the phone."

She sucked in a deep breath and let it out slowly. "Hey, babe," she said. Saying that word felt weird. It wasn't anything she'd ever said to a boyfriend. Cannon had called her that once. But that felt natural. This felt forced.

"Hi, sweetheart. How's my girl doing?" Cannon asked. "Did you have a nice relaxing morning? I hope you used that bubble bath I left out for you."

"Yeah. That was nice." What the fuck was he talking about? First, his tub was tiny and she doubted he had any kind of bath salts or bubbles anywhere in his bachelor pad.

"Good," he said. "I'm sorry Kinley had to cancel on you today."

Oh shit. She swallowed her beating heart. Kinley had done nothing of the sort, but somehow, she must have known there was a problem, but she hadn't come to the door. Or maybe she'd seen something and called Cannon? Or maybe the cop outside?

Jolene could ask herself how Cannon knew that Kinley wasn't there, but that would just be a waste of mind space. She needed the moment. And to know that Cannon was doing something to save her.

She didn't need to know the details.

"I know. That was a bummer, but I've spent some time doing some digging and I've made one very interesting revelation. I think you should come home so we can talk about it."

"I'm only ten minutes away."

"Perfect. I'll see you then."

Justin quickly ended the call. "This is going to be so much fun."

"What are you planning on doing?"

"You haven't figured that out yet?" He stood, yanking her violently to her feet. He grabbed her hair and dragged her toward the kitchen, pressing the gun to her temple.

"Why don't you enlighten me."

He pushed her onto a chair. Holding his weapon in the air, he rummaged through the drawers until he found duct tape. Tugging her hands behind her back, he tied her wrists together. "Just like your father and just like Carl, he's going to watch me have my way with you." Justin leaned closer. His hot breath made the hair on her neck stand on end. "I'm going to treat you like a man should. Take you rough and hard and in ways he would never dare. And then he's going to watch you slowly die. And then, after you've taken your last breath, I'm going to kill him, but it will look like a suicide. It will be a tough one. A decorated military man. Delta Force no less. But this will raise questions on what really happened to his ex-girlfriend. There will be an inquiry and it will get messy and the medical examiner will have to take another look and new evidence will come to light and guess what? It will turn out that Cannon killed Kaylee Ann and Carl."

She wanted to laugh, but that probably wouldn't be a good idea. In all of her years writing about serial killers, many of them had a hand in their own demise because they believed they were untouchable and they developed these grandiose plans that they honestly thought were brilliant.

Well, this one wasn't.

And it would be his downfall.

The only question was would she stay alive long enough to see Cannon take him down and slap some handcuffs on this asshole?

The front door rattled.

She held her breath.

"Looks like the show is about to begin." Justin

kissed her cheek. "Soon, you're going to be begging me to give it to you and you'll love being with a real man. Consider yourself lucky that it will be your last experience here on earth."

* * *

Cannon sucked in a deep breath and twisted the handle on the front door. "Honey, I'm home." He appeared in the doorway and did his best to act as if he were totally surprised by the fact his girlfriend was tied up and Justin stood in the middle of his kitchen waving a gun.

Cannon reached for his weapon.

"I wouldn't do that if I were you." Justin pushed his gun into the side of Jolene's head.

She squinted.

"Come any closer and I'll blow her brains out all over her kitchen." Justin had this wild look about him. His eyes were wide and his pupils dilated.

Cannon caught her gaze as he held his hands up, dangling his gun on his fingertips. He had to trust that Huck, Oz, and Lefty were in place and would enter the house at the right moment. "Why didn't you tell me we had company? I would have brought home a bottle of wine."

Justin snagged the weapon out of Cannon's hand. He set it on the table.

Mistake number one because it wasn't out of reach.

Cannon stared at her, unwilling to tear his gaze away. He could see all that he needed to of Justin out of the corner of his eye. He just wished he could have kept his earpiece in so he could hear his men. But if he had, his cover would have been blown.

"He showed up unannounced," she mumbled.

"That's not very cool. Next time you should call first." He folded his arms. "I'd appreciate it if you untied my girlfriend."

"Have a seat." Justin waved the tape in his free hand. "Let me get you all bound up and I'll release her."

"Are you going to let her go?" Cannon asked.

"Hell no. She and I are going to have a little party and you're going to watch." Justin changed his aim and gave Cannon a little poke in the chest with his gun. "When I was fucking Kaylee Ann, Carl cried like a baby and begged me to stop. But I think Kaylee Ann enjoyed it. No. I know she did. She had an orgasm like—"

Cannon cocked his fist and raised his arm.

Justin took the butt of his weapon and smacked him on the side of the face.

"Fuck," Cannon muttered. "That hurt."

"Next time it will be Jolene who will have to pay for your mistakes. Now sit down and be quiet."

When Cannon had entered the house, he'd turned on the security cameras so his team could see everything that was going on inside, but they couldn't hear anything. But having a visual allowed them to have a plan of attack and right about now, he hoped they were climbing through a bedroom window. Now he just had to get Justin's back to the hallway.

Cannon pulled the chair toward him and made sure he adjusted it just enough so that when Justin tied his hands, Justin's back would be toward the bedroom. Cannon wouldn't be able to see if his plan worked, but he trusted his team with his life. He glanced in Jolene's direction. Tears flowed freely down her cheeks.

"It's going to be okay," he said softly.

"You can tell her that all you want, but she knows she's going to—umph. What the hell?" Justin whipped around before he had the chance to wrap any tape around Cannon's wrists.

Cannon jumped to his feet, knocking over the chair. He spun.

"Drop your weapon, asshole," Lefty said.

Huck appeared in the hallway. "Do what he says. This house is surrounded."

Oz came barreling through the front door.

Cannon let out a long breath as he raced to Jolene's side. He quickly found a knife and cut her from her restraints. "Are you okay? Did he touch you? Hurt you? I'll kick the shit out of him if he did."

She reached out and touched her fingers to his cheek.

He winced. "You're bleeding," she whispered.

"I'm fine."

She glanced to her left.

He followed her gaze. Tate had come in the house and was reading Justin his rights as he was eerily quiet.

"He killed my parents and he killed Kaylee Ann and Carl," she said.

"I know." He cupped her face, kissing her forehead. "But it's over."

"He wants me to write his story. That's what this was all about." She curled her fingers around Cannon's wrists. "I need to say something to him."

"Are you sure?"

"I'm positive."

Cannon took a step back. "I'm right here." He had no idea what she was going to say, but he could tell by the pure look of determination in her eyes that whatever it was, it was incredibly important to her, and he wasn't about to stand in her way.

Every muscle in Jolene's body trembled. Not from fear. Not anymore. He'd terrorized her long before she knew his identity. She'd given this man power over her life ever since her parents had died.

But no more.

He'd been captured and now she held the power and she could control the one thing that mattered the most.

His story.

Other writers might want to tell it and she might not be able to talk them into their silence, but she could keep hers. And she knew Cannon would keep his.

And probably everyone in this room.

She inched closer to Justin who had the audacity to smile.

"You think this is over? Because it's not. There

isn't enough evidence to pin anything on me but this," Justin said.

"That's where you're wrong," Cannon chimed in. "Just so you know, the medical examiner turned on you, and all sorts of evidence has turned up. You'll never get out of prison. We'll see to that."

Justin narrowed his glare. "You're lying."

"No. He's not and the best part is I'm never going to allow myself to be interviewed or speak publicly about this case. The only thing I'm going to do is testify in court. You are never going to get a story out of me. No crime book. No podcast. No nothing. You will never get my attention. You're not worth it."

"What about the victims? Don't you want to tell their stories?" Justin asked. "Isn't that the focus of everything you do?"

"You can't manipulate me." She poked him in the chest. "And yes. I do want to tell their stories, but it doesn't have to be about who murdered them. Or how their lives ended. It will be about how we can celebrate who they were. I can do that without ever mentioning you or what you did." She squared her shoulders. "Now, can you please get this piece of shit out of my boyfriend's house."

"Gladly," Tate said.

"We'll be outside." Lefty patted Cannon on the back.

Once the house was clear, Jolene fell into Cannon's arms. She had no tears left to cry. She just wanted to be held.

"That was not how I expected my day to go," she said.

He ran his hands up and down her back. "I shouldn't have left you. I'm sorry about that."

"You came back and you saved me."

"I had a little help." He cupped her chin. "Am I really your boyfriend?"

"I was hoping that maybe we could give this a go. I mean, I can write anywhere and I like a change of scenery. I wouldn't mind coming down here when you're not deployed."

"When I have time off, I can come to Virginia."

"Are we nuts?"

"Probably," he whispered.

"I do have one request that could be a deal breaker."

"What's that?"

"The decor in this place has to change and you will need to provide me with some bubble bath."

He laughed. "I rent this place and the lease is up

in a couple of months, so I can find something with a bigger tub and you can pick out the furniture."

"And the artwork because that dog poker party has got to go."

He groaned. "Yes, ma'am." He kissed her. Hard. It was the kind of kiss that told her he wasn't ever going to let her go and she didn't want him to. "I'm falling hard for you, Jolene."

"Not as hard as I am for you."

Jolene leaned against the kitchen counter in Cannon's new house and chewed on her fingernail while Lefty and Kinley thumbed through the draft of her latest book. She normally didn't stand there and watch people skim her work, but they insisted.

She wished Cannon would hurry up and finish mowing the damn lawn. He'd run outside like a bat out of hell when the duo had shown up. Of course, he'd been deployed for ten days and the lawn seriously needed some tender loving care.

He'd only just moved and there were boxes everywhere. She planned on moving in next month as soon as she took care of some loose ends up in Virginia. She never thought she'd leave her hometown. She'd always believed she had some cosmic connection to the state because of her parents' murders, but it hadn't been that at all.

And now that Justin was facing life in prison without the possibility of parole, it didn't matter where she lived. Maybe it never did, but now that she'd found her soulmate, she only wanted to be wherever he was and right now, that was Killeen, Texas.

"This is amazing." Kinley wiped a single tear that rolled down her cheek as she looked up. "You really captured what I was feeling and going through during the entire time."

"I tried to channel your emotions," Jolene said.

"You did just that." Lefty stood. "I have to tell you that I was skeptical when Kinley told me she wanted to do this, but I'm excited for the final product."

"I'm pleased you like it." Jolene let out a sigh of relief. Their approval meant the world to her.

"Cannon tells me that you're still refusing to discuss publicly Justin and your story. Are you sure you want to do that?" Kinley took her husband's hand.

"Yes," Jolene said. "It would give that monster too much satisfaction. Maybe when he's dead, but not while he still has oxygen in his lungs."

"I can respect that," Lefty said. "Thanks for letting us give our approval on the draft."

Kinley leaned in and gave Jolene a hug. "We better be going. Besides, Cannon is annoyed we showed up so soon considering you just landed a few hours ago."

"He'll get over it." It dawned on her that in the two hours she'd been sitting with Kinley and her husband, the lawn mower engine hadn't been making any noise at all. She walked them to the front door and pulled it open. "We'll all have to get together for dinner before Cannon and I drive to Virginia to get my shit."

"We'd love that," Lefty said as he stepped into the front yard.

Cannon jumped from his chair on the front porch. "Leaving so soon?"

Lefty laughed. "Later, man."

"I thought you were going to mow the lawn?" She slid her arm low around his waist and waved to their friends as they drove away.

"I didn't want to be all sweaty when they left." He pressed his lips against her temple. "I've missed you. I'm so happy you agreed to move here with me. I know it's still going to be hard with deployments, but we'll be together more."

She glanced up and smiled. "I love you."

He took her chin with his thumb and forefinger. "I love you so much I went out and did this." He stuffed his hand in his pocket and pulled out a small box.

"Oh my God." She covered her mouth. "That isn't what I think it is," she whispered.

He lowered himself to one knee and opened the small velvet case. A sparkling diamond ring shimmered in the sun.

"I had no idea that when I agreed to pick you up at the airport that you'd steal my heart. But you did and I want to spend the rest of my life showing you just how much I love you." He took the ring from the box and placed it on her shaky finger.

A few happy tears scorched a path down her cheek.

"Will you do me the honor of being my wife?"

"Yes," she said. "A million times, yes."

He stood. "The neighbors are staring," he whispered as he pressed his lips over hers in a brief kiss.

"It's because our yard looks like shit."

He laughed. "I see how it's going to be in this marriage."

She wrapped her arms around his strong shoulders. When she'd first come to Texas it was for a story. She never thought she'd find the man who'd not only help her find closure to her past, but who would be her present and her future.

Thank you for taking the time to read *Shielding Jolene*. Please feel free to leave an HONEST review. *Sign up for my Newsletter (https://dl.bookfunnel.com/ 82gm8b9k4y) where I often give away free books before publication.*

Join my private Facebook group (https://www.facebook. com/groups/191706547909047/) where I post exclusive excerpts and discuss all things murder and love!

Never miss a new release. Follow me on
Amazon:amazon.com/author/jentalty
And on Bookbub: bookbub.com/authors/jen-talty

COLOR ME YOURS

COLOR ME SMART

COLOR ME FREE

COLOR ME LUCKY

COLOR ME ICE

It's all in the Whiskey

JOHNNIE WALKER

GEORGIA MOON

JACK DANIELS

JIM BEAM

WHISKEY SOUR

WHISKEY COBBLER

WHISKEY SMASH

Search and Rescue

PROTECTING AINSLEY

PROTECTING CLOVER

PROTECTING OLYMPIA

PROTECTING FREEDOM

PROTECTING PRINCESS

NY STATE TROOPER SERIES

In Two Weeks

Dark Water

Deadly Secrets

Murder in paradise Bay

To Protect His own

Deadly Seduction

When A Stranger Calls

His Deadly Past

The Corkscrew Killer

Brand New Novella for the First Responders series

A spin off from the NY State Troopers series

PLAYING WITH FIRE

PRIVATE CONVERSATION

THE RIGHT GROOM

AFTER THE FIRE

CAUGHT IN THE FLAMES

The Men of Thief Lake

REKINDLED

DESTINY'S DREAM

Federal Investigators

JANE DOE'S RETURN

THE BUTTERFLY MURDERS

The Aegis Network

THE LIGHTHOUSE

HER LAST HOPE

THE LAST FLIGHT

THE RETURN HOME

THE MATRIARCH

The Collective Order

THE LOST SISTER

THE LOST SOLDIER

THE LOST SOUL

THE LOST CONNECTION

A Spin-Off Series: Witches Academy Series

THE NEW ORDER

Special Forces Operation Alpha

BURNING DESIRE

BURNING KISS

BURNING SKIES

BURNING LIES

BURNING HEART

BURNING BED

REMEMBER ME ALWAYS

The Brotherhood Protectors

Out of the Wild

ROUGH JUSTICE

ROUGH AROUND THE EDGES

ROUGH RIDE

ROUGH EDGE

ROUGH BEAUTY

The Brotherhood Protectors

The Saving Series

SAVING LOVE

SAVING MAGNOLIA

SAVING LEATHER

Hot Hunks

Cove's Blind Date Blows Up

My Everyday Hero – Ledger

Tempting Tavor

Holiday Romances

A CHRISTMAS GETAWAY

ALASKAN CHRISTMAS

WHISPERS

CHRISTMAS IN THE SAND

CHRISTMAS IN JULY

Heroes & Heroines on the Field

TAKING A RISK

TEE TIME

A New Dawn

THE BLIND DATE

SPRING FLING

SUMMER'S GONE

WINTER WEDDING

Witches and Werewolves

LADY SASS

ALL THAT SASS

Jen Talty is the *USA Today* Bestselling Author of Contemporary Romance, Romantic Suspense, and Paranormal Romance. In the fall of 2020, her short story was selected and featured in a 1001 Dark Nights Anthology. She is currently contracted to write a new series with Kristen Proby's Lady Boss Press, as well as Susan Stoker's *Special Forces: Operation Alpha* and Elle James's *Brotherhood Protectors*.

Regardless of the genre, her goal is to take you on a ride that will leave you floating under the sun with warmth in your heart. She writes stories about broken heroes and heroines who aren't necessarily looking for romance, but in the end, they find the kind of love books are written about :).

She first started writing while carting her kids to one hockey rink after the other, averaging 170 games per year between 3 kids in 2 countries and 5 states. Her first book, IN TWO WEEKS was originally published in 2007. In 2010 she helped form a publishing company (Cool Gus Publishing) with *NY Times* Bestselling Author Bob Mayer where she ran the technical side of the business through 2016.

Jen is currently enjoying the next phase of her life… the empty nester! She and her husband reside in Jupiter, Florida.

Grab a glass of vino, kick back, relax, and let the romance roll in…

Sign up for my Newsletter (https://dl.bookfunnel.com/ 82gm8b9k4y) where I often give away free books before publication.

Join my private Facebook group (https://www.facebook. com/groups/1917065479047/) where I post exclusive excerpts and discuss all things murder and love!

Never miss a new release. Follow me on Amazon:amazon.com/author/jentalty

And on Bookbub: bookbub.com/authors/jen-talty

There are many more books in this fan fiction world than listed here, for an up-to-date list go to www.AcesPress.com

You can also visit our Amazon page at:
http://www.amazon.com/author/operationalpha

Special Forces: Operation Alpha World
Christie Adams: Charity's Heart
Denise Agnew: Dangerous to Hold
Shauna Allen: Awakening Aubrey
Brynne Asher: Blackburn
Linzi Baxter: Unlocking Dreams
Jennifer Becker: Hiding Catherine
Alice Bello: Shadowing Milly
Heather Blair: Rescue Me
Misha Blake: Flash
Anna Blakely: Rescuing Gracelynn
Julia Bright: Saving Lorelei
Cara Carnes: Protecting Mari
Kendra Mei Chailyn: Beast
Melissa Kay Clarke: Rescuing Annabeth
Samantha A. Cole: Handling Haven
Sue Coletta: Hacked
Melissa Combs: Gallant
Lorelei Confer: Protecting Sara

Anne Conley: Redemption for Misty

KaLyn Cooper: Rescuing Melina

Janie Crouch: Storm

Liz Crowe: Marking Mariah

Sarah Curtis: Securing the Odds

Jordan Dane: Redemption for Avery

Tarina Deaton: Found in the Lost

Aspen Drake, Intense

KL Donn: Unraveling Love

Riley Edwards: Protecting Olivia

PJ Fiala: Defending Sophie

Nicole Flockton: Protecting Maria

Alexa Gregory: Backdraft

Michele Gwynn: Rescuing Emma

Casey Hagen: Shielding Nebraska

Desiree Holt: Protecting Maddie

Kathy Ivan: Saving Sarah

Kris Jacen, Be With Me

Jesse Jacobson: Protecting Honor

Silver James: Rescue Moon

Becca Jameson: Saving Sofia

Kate Kinsley: Protecting Ava

Rayne Lewis: Justice for Mary

Heather Long: Securing Arizona

Gennita Low: No Protection

Kirsten Lynn: Joining Forces for Jesse

Jenika Snow: Protecting Lily

Lynne St. James: SEAL's Spitfire

Dee Stewart: Conner

Harley Stone: Rescuing Mercy

Sarah Stone: Shielding Grace

Jen Talty: Burning Desire

Reina Torres, Rescuing Hi'ilani

Savvi V: Loving Lex

Megan Vernon: Protecting Us

LJ Vickery: Circus Comes to Town

Rachel Young: Because of Marissa

R. C. Wynne: Shadows Renewed

Delta Team Three Series

Lori Ryan: Nori's Delta

Becca Jameson: Destiny's Delta

Lynne St James, Gwen's Delta

Elle James: Ivy's Delta

Riley Edwards: Hope's Delta

Police and Fire: Operation Alpha World

Freya Barker: Burning for Autumn

B.P. Beth: Scott

Jane Blythe: Salvaging Marigold

Julia Bright, Justice for Amber

Anna Brooks, Guarding Georgia

KaLyn Cooper: Justice for Gwen
Aspen Drake: Sheltering Emma
Emily Gray: Shelter for Allegra
Alexa Gregory: Backdraft
Deanndra Hall: Shelter for Sharla
Barb Han: Kace
EM Hayes: Gambling for Ashleigh
India Kells: Shadow Killer
CM Steele: Guarding Hope
Reina Torres: Justice for Sloane
Aubree Valentine, Justice for Danielle
Maddie Wade: Finding English
Stacey Wilk: Stage Fright
Laine Vess: Justice for Lauren

Tarpley VFD Series

Silver James, Fighting for Elena
Deanndra Hall, Fighting for Carly
Haven Rose, Fighting for Calliope
MJ Nightingale, Fighting for Jemma
TL Reeve, Fighting for Brittney
Nicole Flockton, Fighting for Nadia

As you know, this book included at least one character from Susan Stoker's books. To check out more, see below.

SEAL Team Hawaii Series

Finding Elodie

Finding Lexie

Finding Kenna (Oct 2021)

Finding Monica (May 2022)

Finding Carly (TBA)

Finding Ashlyn (TBA)

Finding Jodelle (TBA)

Eagle Point Search & Rescue

Searching for Lilly (Mar 2022)

Searching for Elsie (Jun 2022)

Searching for Bristol (Nov 2022)

Searching for Caryn (TBA)

Searching for Finley (TBA)

Searching for Heather (TBA)

Searching for Khloe (TBA)

The Refuge Series

Deserving Alaska (Aug 2022)

Deserving Henley (Jan 2023)

Deserving Reese (TBA)
Deserving Cora (TBA)
Deserving Lara (TBA)
Deserving Maisy (TBA)
Deserving Ryleigh (TBA)

Delta Team Two Series
Shielding Gillian
Shielding Kinley
Shielding Aspen
Shielding Jayme (novella)
Shielding Riley
Shielding Devyn
Shielding Ember
Shielding Sierra (Jan 2022)

SEAL of Protection: Legacy Series
Securing Caite (FREE!)
Securing Brenae (novella)
Securing Sidney
Securing Piper
Securing Zoey
Securing Avery
Securing Kalee
Securing Jane

Delta Force Heroes Series
Rescuing Rayne (FREE!)
Rescuing Aimee (novella)
Rescuing Emily
Rescuing Harley
Marrying Emily (novella)
Rescuing Kassie
Rescuing Bryn
Rescuing Casey
Rescuing Sadie (novella)
Rescuing Wendy
Rescuing Mary
Rescuing Macie (novella)
Rescuing Annie (Feb 2022)

Badge of Honor: Texas Heroes Series
Justice for Mackenzie (FREE!)
Justice for Mickie
Justice for Corrie
Justice for Laine (novella)
Shelter for Elizabeth
Justice for Boone
Shelter for Adeline
Shelter for Sophie
Justice for Erin
Justice for Milena

Shelter for Blythe
Justice for Hope
Shelter for Quinn
Shelter for Koren
Shelter for Penelope

SEAL of Protection Series
Protecting Caroline (FREE!)
Protecting Alabama
Protecting Fiona
Marrying Caroline (novella)
Protecting Summer
Protecting Cheyenne
Protecting Jessyka
Protecting Julie (novella)
Protecting Melody
Protecting the Future
Protecting Kiera (novella)
Protecting Alabama's Kids (novella)
Protecting Dakota

New York Times, USA Today and *Wall Street Journal* Bestselling Author Susan Stoker has a heart as big as the state of Tennessee where she lives, but this all American girl has also spent the last fourteen years living in Missouri, California, Colorado, Indiana, and Texas. She's married to a retired Army man who now gets to follow *her* around the country.

www.stokeraces.com
www.AcesPress.com
susan@stokeraces.com

Made in United States
Cleveland, OH
27 September 2025